You're Pregnant," Ryan Declared, Thinking It Was Impossible— Knowing It Wasn't.

When Ashley gasped, he knew he was right.

"This doesn't concern you," she told him.

"Who's the father?" he asked, his voice cold and harsh.

"I'm not telling you."

He stepped closer to her. "You know I can find out. I have enough money to get any information I want."

Suddenly she looked frightened. Stunned, he could only stare at her. "There isn't another man, is there?" he asked.

Ashley was going to have a baby. *His* baby....

Dear Reader,

The story posed an interesting question to me:

What happens when an aggressive man, who is accustomed to getting what he wants, clashes with a beautiful woman, who has her own ideas about how she will live her life? It's a juicy dilemma when these two battle it out, even while bonding in a fiery attraction that escalates every second they are together.

Does love have a chance to bloom under such conditions? When two strong wills clash, how can there be a happy ending?

It was exciting to write about a woman whose heart would not melt over a handsome millionaire who was determined to be part of her life. Sparks fly with Ryan and Ashley, starting fires that burn away old notions and change both their lives.

I hope, dear reader, that you enjoy meeting Ryan and Ashley and following their rocky journey to love.

Sara Orwig

SARA ORWIG

PREGNANT AT THE WEDDING

Published by Silhouette Books
America's Publisher of Contemporary Romance

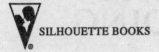

SILHOUETTE BOOKS

ISBN-13: 978-0-373-76864-6
ISBN-10:   0-373-76864-8

PREGNANT AT THE WEDDING

Copyright © 2008 by Sara Orwig

This edition published by arrangement with Harlequin Books S.A.

® and TM are trademarks of Harlequin Books S.A., used under license. Trademarks indicated with ® are registered in the United States Patent and Trademark Office, the Canadian Trade Marks Office and in other countries.

Visit Silhouette Books at www.eHarlequin.com

Printed in U.S.A.

SARA ORWIG

lives in Oklahoma. She has a patient husband, who will take her on research trips anywhere, from big cities to old forts. She is an avid collector of Western history books. With a master's degree in English, Sara has written historical romance, mainstream fiction and contemporary romance. Books are beloved treasures that take Sara to magical worlds, and she loves both reading and writing them.

With thanks to MJ for some fabulous moments, plus so many other reasons, and thanks to Demetria, who has a multitude of ideas. Special thanks to my chums, Hannah Ellen, Rachel, Elisabeth, Colin and Cameron for joy.

One

What was he doing here? The moment Ashley Smith dreaded, dreamed about, worried over for months and then convinced herself wouldn't occur had finally happened.

As the bride and groom circled the floor for their first dance at an exclusive Dallas country club, Ashley's satisfaction over the smoothly flowing wedding reception vanished. Beyond the newly married couple, standing in the crowd of guests, was tall, black-haired Ryan Warner. *The* Ryan Warner, millionaire owner of the Warner hotel chain. The man she'd had a wild, passionate weekend with almost four months ago.

As the past assaulted Ashley, her head swam. Her first instinct was to run, but as the wedding planner, she had to stay to see that all the events flowed smoothly.

Even while dread filled her, she still thought that Ryan was the most handsome man she had ever known.

Her heart thudded when she remembered his mouth on hers.

Staring at Ryan, she would never understand what had overcome her that weekend—except his sexy appeal and spellbinding charm. Never before in her life had she cut loose like that. Hot kisses, magical hands, irresistible seduction—memories of Ryan flashed in her mind. She recalled his take-charge manner and his fascinating charisma. After they'd made love, she'd been stunned and embarrassed by her actions.

Now here he was, just yards away across the ballroom, with a drink in his hand. Women smiled at him while he watched the bride and groom dance. Suddenly, Ashley was conscious of herself in her pale yellow linen suit, yellow silk blouse and matching pumps. She smoothed her skirt and tucked a stray strand of her blond hair in place.

She hadn't seen Ryan's name on the guest list. If she had known he would be here, she would have given the job to her assistant today. Ryan Warner was the last person on earth she wanted to encounter. So far, he hadn't seen her and she hoped to keep it that way.

If at all possible, she hoped to avoid him. She did not want to renew her acquaintance with him. At least, not until she was ready to deal with him. Though he didn't know it, he was involved in the enormous secret she kept from her family.

Her gaze drifted over the crowd again. At four inches over six feet tall, Ryan was easy to find. He was dancing now, with a gorgeous brunette, and to Ashley's relief, he seemed focused on his partner. Ashley prayed he had arrived with the woman and would soon leave with her.

Ashley melted into the crowd, glancing occasionally at Ryan while she moved around the room. Reassured the reception was progressing smoothly, she checked that the waiters picked up empty glasses, serving dishes were filled and guests seemed to be enjoying themselves.

Ashley had another brief surge of reassurance that the wedding and reception were going off without a hitch as she made her way toward the newly married couple. Emily and Jake Thorne looked radiant, both glowing, with constant smiles. She thought they looked the perfect couple together—a beautiful, brown-haired bride with her tall, black-haired, handsome husband. During the early stages of planning the elaborate wedding and reception, Emily had confided in Ashley that her union with Jake was a marriage of convenience. Ashley had soothed her client's jitters and doubts, and now gave herself a mental pat on the back for helping to make this day great for them and a time to remember the rest of their lives.

Finally, it was time to cut the cake, and the second the next dance stopped, Ashley approached the bride. "Cake-cutting time," she stated. "I have the photographer ready and waiting."

"Thanks, Ashley. This is wonderful!" Emily gushed.

"I'm glad. By the way, I don't recall Ryan Warner's name on the guest list," she added casually.

Emily shrugged. "Ryan and Jake and our best man, Nick Colton, are the closest of friends. They all grew up together. Ryan was in Europe and tied up in business and said he couldn't make the wedding, but then he surprised us this morning, and here he is. Do you know—"

"There's the photographer," Ashley interrupted, having another rush of apprehension. "Go get some great pictures!" She hurried away, relieved that soon all eyes would be on the bride and groom.

Certain nothing would go wrong with the photographer

and that cutting the cake would be uneventful, Ashley rushed to the powder room to get herself together. Jake still had to throw Emily's garter and she had to toss her bouquet, but little by little, they were getting through the reception. It would be over soon, but not soon enough.

When Ashley rejoined the crowd, the band still played and couples danced. She didn't see Ryan and, praying he had left the reception, she hurried to check on the tables of food. She was looking at the swan ice sculpture on the center table when a hand wrapped lightly around her wrist.

"Well, hello," said a deep voice, and her heart missed a beat.

She turned to look into curious green eyes, eyes fringed with thick black lashes beneath a head of wavy black hair. Eyes as green as a meadow and sexy enough to make her pulse jump. It was those unforgettable eyes that could wreak havoc with her insides.

"What are you doing here?" he asked. "Do you know Emily and Jake?"

"Yes, I do. It's nice to see you," she said, intending to escape, aware he still was holding her wrist lightly. With his hand there, he might be able to feel her racing pulse.

"Let's dance," Ryan said, drawing her the few steps toward the dance floor. Dressed in a navy suit and white shirt, he stood out in the crowd of other well-dressed men. She suspected that it was due to an aura of self-assurance and his commanding manner.

"I can't dance today. I'm the wedding planner and I'm working."

"I knew you were a wedding planner. It didn't occur to me that you might be hired to do this wedding."

"When I'm working, I don't dance," she said, pulling back slightly as they walked a few more steps to the dance floor. She didn't want to make a scene, yet she knew she had to get away from him.

"Nonsense," he said, smiling at her and taking her into his arms.

Even though she hoped to escape, she couldn't keep from noticing his firm jaw, prominent cheekbones, straight nose and broad shoulders. She remembered the last with absolute clarity—shoulders that were muscled, and a chest that was rock hard. She recalled everything about him in detail. As her face flushed, a mixture of emotions battled in her.

She had to get him out of her life, and the sooner, the better. Memories of his kisses taunted her as her gaze drifted over his features. When his attention lowered to her mouth, her breath caught.

"You ran out on me," he said, steadily watching her.

"Yes, well, that weekend was a mistake I've regretted terribly."

"Ouch! You didn't seem so unhappy at the time," he said, studying her.

"It was uncharacteristic for me. I've never...never let go like that. Frankly, I'm working, and I'd rather not discuss it," she said, wishing her voice was firmer, too aware of each time their legs brushed.

"You look as beautiful as I remember," he said in his deep voice, and she grew warmer, pleased in spite of her concerns.

"How many women have you said that to recently?" she asked. "Look, I need—"

"No, you don't. The reception is going great and the bride and groom are having a blast. Relax and enjoy a dance with me. Uncharacteristic or not, why did you run out like that?"

"I just told you the reason. I meant it."

"Then you had a big change of heart, because for forty-eight hours, we got along great. The best," he said in a deeper voice, and she knew he was remembering when they had made love.

"That's over," she said. Ashley wondered where the firmness in her voice had gone and why he had such a potent effect on her.

"You don't say," he murmured. "I hunted for you, but there wasn't any A. Smith, wedding planner listed in the phone book."

"I don't have a landline," she said, thinking how civilized they were behaving. At the same time, she was torn between wanting to kiss him and wanting to run from him.

"And here my buddy Jake hired you and has been working with you."

"Actually, I've worked more with Emily."

"Maybe, but Jake knew about you. It never occurred to me to ask him about his wedding planner. I'm not into weddings much."

"You made that clear at the time,"

He grinned. "At least you haven't forgotten me."

"That's impossible," she snapped, and one of his dark eyebrows arched in question.

"Why do I get the feeling that there is something wrong here?" he asked her with an intense scrutiny that worried her.

"Because something is the matter. I told you that I'm working. I shouldn't be dancing."

"I don't think that's it," he said, and she looked away, thinking he was far too perceptive. His arm tightened around her waist, drawing her closer.

She was acutely conscious of their physical contact, her hand in his warm hand, her other hand on his shoulder while they moved together. She looked up at him, hating that each time she gazed into his eyes, her heartbeat quickened.

"Look, that weekend we had is over." He spun her around and danced her into a corner. "I've moved on with my life," she added.

"I don't usually strike out like this," he said, still studying her. "I want to talk to you," he stated in a low voice, drawing her nearer to him.

"Look, I need—"

"I thought we both had a great time. I got the impression that you were as happy with the situation as I was."

"I told you, I sort of lost myself that weekend," she said, as she wriggled away from him, taking a step back to put more distance between them. Even still, he was too close. His mouth was only inches from hers. Half of her wanted to stand on tiptoe and kiss him, and the other half wanted to break and run. The sensible half *needed* to get away, and she tried to concentrate on doing that as quickly as possible. What was it about him that scrambled her cool logic so badly?

"I thought our time together was fantastic, and I've missed you and searched for you," he insisted in a thicker voice that turned her insides to jelly.

"I'm sorry," she replied, remembering her reasons for wanting to avoid him, determined to end the conversation. "I may have ruffled your ego, but I've seen pictures of you—just recently with a gorgeous redhead on your arm. You haven't been pining away, without me. It's over. You may not be accustomed to hearing that, but get it through your head."

"You're saying it's over," he replied, "but what's wrong with renewing our acquaintance?" He took her wrist once more, and she knew he could feel her revealing heartbeat.

"If that makes you happy, I'll admit that I physically respond to you. But I have a job to do now."

"This is a big puzzle," he said, moving nearer again and wrapping his arm around her waist. Her gaze lowered to his full and sensual lips, and she remembered his fantastic kisses.

"I can see from your big blue eyes that you haven't forgotten that weekend. I don't think you regret it as much as you're saying," he added softly.

"Oh, yes, I do!" she whispered, knowing she should walk away from him. But she simply stood there, mesmerized by his intense gaze. He was looking at her as if she were the only woman on earth.

"Okay, you're working now. When this is over, go to dinner with me and let's talk. Surely you can give me that much of your time," he said with a faint smile.

Ashley paused, unable to tell him a lie, yet wanting to.

"There," he said, as if she'd already agreed. "If I thought I was being intrusive and you couldn't stand me, I wouldn't insist, but you're as breathless as I am." His rich, deep voice was as tangible as a caress. "If nothing else, let's go to dinner and see what happens."

"Nothing will occur."

His eyebrow arched wickedly. "You don't know that for sure. Let my imagination have its own good time. When are you through working this reception?"

"When the bride and groom leave. My assistant is here, and the cleanup crew are experienced and know what to do."

"Great! So you'll go with me then."

"I don't see any point—"

"There's a definite point," he said. "It makes me incredibly happy. You won't shatter my ego—"

She received a wide grin from him that tempted her to respond. "That's impossible."

"Ah, I think I see a glimmer of a smile," he said, leaning down to peer at her.

"Now you've gotten your way," she replied.

"Only about dinner," he said. "There's a whole lot more I want."

Ashley drew a deep breath. The way he pulled on her senses was irresistible, magnetic. She had no control over how her body responded. She couldn't understand her own reactions. He was so unreservedly autocratic, yet at the same time charismatic...

"I need to return to work."

"You do recall our weekend together?" he asked softly. "It was one of the best I ever had."

"It was a long time ago," she said stiffly. "I'm going back to work." She turned toward the dance floor and he hurried after her, holding her arm as they joined the other guests.

"I need to see about the bride," she told him.

"I'll find you when they leave."

"Fine. I'll be around," she said.

"You sound as if I'm going to haul you to jail instead of take you to dinner," he added lightly. Yet he gazed at her intently, and she could see the curiosity in his expression.

She realized the more she tried to get rid of him, the more interested he became. "I think you're unaccustomed to hearing no."

"I have to admit that I'm curious why. We can talk about it later. Go do what you have to do now."

"I see you two know each other," Nick Colton said, joining them and turning to Ashley. "And I saw you dancing with Ryan. Now I'd like a turn." He moved forward to place himself between the pair.

Just as she was about to decline, Ryan moved closer, putting a possessive arm around her shoulder. "We're very old and good friends. Ashley really can't dance while she's on the job. You're out of luck this time."

It was on the tip of her tongue to object when Emily touched her arm. "Please excuse me, both of you," Ashley said, turning to the bride and wishing she had avoided letting Ryan talk her into a dinner date.

"The photographer is asking about me tossing my bouquet," Emily said.

"It's time, and you rescued me from dancing when I have other things to do. Ryan doesn't take refusal well."

An hour later, Emily told Ashley that she and Jake would be leaving soon. Ashley asked her brown-haired assistant, Jenna Fremont, to take over. Then Ashley left, wondering if she was making a huge mistake.

Another first caused by Ryan. She had never run from someone before, and she felt terrible one minute and relieved the next. If he really wanted to see her, he knew how to find her now. But she suspected another quick departure from her would turn him off for good. Men like Ryan did not chase after women who didn't want to see them. They were probably accustomed to females chasing after them.

At her duplex apartment in a gated area, Ashley spent the evening thinking about Ryan. She couldn't get him out of her thoughts, and in some ways, she was disappointed she wasn't with him.

She remembered with clarity the excitement she'd had with him, as well as the reasons she had wanted to get away from him.

Early that Sunday morning when they had been together, Ashley had awakened to find him missing. She'd wrapped herself in a towel and gone looking for him, stopping in her tracks when she heard low voices. He'd been arguing with a woman.

Ashley had known he was a millionaire playboy, so she shouldn't have been surprised by the presence of a woman.

But suddenly, she realized just how stupid she was in giving herself to him completely that wild weekend. Dressing swiftly, she'd gathered her things. While he still talked, she had slipped out a back door, getting away from his condo as quickly as possible and into the taxi she'd called from her cell phone. They hadn't had contact since then—until today.

Finding it difficult to get to sleep now, she tossed and turned. When she finally did doze, she dreamed of Ryan and being in his arms again.

The next day, while she tried to do chores she had put off in the last hectic days of getting ready for the Carlisle-Thorne marriage, she couldn't shake him out of her thoughts.

No matter what she did, Ryan was there in her mind.

They had nothing in common. She was a farm girl who'd come to the city and gotten a job. She was sending some of her paycheck home to help her family, because of her father's poor health and financial troubles from a flood last year. Her brother had given up his college education to work on the farm full-time, too. Ryan's world was light-years away from hers. He was a multimillionaire, a self-made man who moved in international circles. He usually had a beautiful socialite with him and lived a jet-set life.

She was amazed he'd even noticed her when they'd met at a party, yet she had fallen into his arms and into his bed with complete abandon. So why wouldn't he have had a pleasurable weekend that he wanted to prolong?

Recalling the large party, for a charity event at a Dallas country club, she remembered how a waiter had slipped while carrying a tray filled with glasses of champagne. Strong arms had caught her to pull her out of the way, and she'd looked up into Ryan's green eyes and been captivated. The attraction was hot, instant and intense. They'd made introductions. They had flirted, talked, and he had charmed her. Eventually she'd told the friends she had come with to leave without her because Ryan would take her home. They had gone to his condo, and in another hour, she had been in his arms, and later, in his bed. She had given her body to him intimately, had explored his and shared her life, even telling him what desperate financial straits her family was in, and how she was helping them. Why had she been so free and open in every possible way with Ryan? He had seduced her and won her total trust.

Disgusted with herself, she tried to stop thinking about him now, finally getting out her bank statements and checking her entries and withdrawals for her business that month. She wrote her regular monthly check to her father, which included every penny she could spare.

When she finished, she spent another restless night, before going to work Monday morning.

Ashley tried to immerse herself in business, meeting a client, setting up appointments, talking to a caterer and a florist. Her day passed, but she constantly became distracted, lost her train of thought and realized she was staring into space, remembering Ryan.

She hadn't seen or heard anything from him since Saturday at the reception, and she decided he'd moved on with his life and she'd seen the last of him. It was for the best.

When it was almost closing time, she walked through her office and headed for the front to ask Carlotta, her receptionist, about an appointment. Carlotta was momentarily on the phone, and Ashley moved away from the desk to wait for her to finish her call. When she glanced out the front window, she saw a black sports car whip into a parking space. The door swung open and Ryan stepped out.

Ashley's insides clenched. Dressed in navy slacks, a white shirt and navy tie, he was as handsome as ever. Wind blew locks of his black hair away from his forehead, and his long-legged stride revealed confidence and purpose.

Ashley knew she didn't want a confrontation with Ryan with an audience, so she hurried to the door and stepped outside. She was oblivious to the bright sunshine, the sweet scents of blossoming fruit trees, the enticing splash of the nearby fountain. She focused totally on the determined male striding toward her. Squaring her shoulders, she walked to meet him, knowing she had to convince him that she'd meant what she'd said to him at the wedding.

She had to send him packing. How difficult it would be! Every square inch of her wanted to be in his arms. She wanted his kisses, and as she watched him striding toward her, she struggled with her inclination to hurry and meet him and do whatever he wanted.

Except she knew she could do no such thing, and as she faced him, she could already feel the clash of wills. Someday, she knew she would have to tell him the truth, but not this soon. Now, she wanted life on her own terms, and she didn't want someone forceful like Ryan meddling in her decisions.

She clenched her fists, reminding herself to stay firm with him. He must not find out the truth so soon. She was carrying his baby from that wild weekend of lust, and she wanted to deal with this secret herself as long as she possibly could.

She stepped forward to meet him, folding her arms across her middle, standing with her feet slightly spread, as if ready for a confrontation. "Why are you here?"

Two

Ryan's green eyes danced with amusement. "Hi, to you, too." Even though he smiled and his voice was cheerful, he watched her intently.

"Ryan, I told you that I don't want to see you."

"So you did, but then you turned right around and promised you'd go to dinner with me," he said. "And I do recall your racing pulse when we were together. There's a conflict between what you say and how you say it. And a few other things."

"I'm trying to do the sensible thing here," she said, conscious that they were probably drawing the attention of her employees. "I've done the nonsense thing with you, now I'm doing otherwise."

"Maybe. By the way, you look as gorgeous as ever," he murmured, studying her and then meeting her gaze. "Whenever I see you, you look great. Luscious," he added softly.

"Thank you," she replied solemnly. His compliments warmed her, and she wanted to smile in return, but didn't. "I'm in the middle of work."

"I called this morning and your receptionist said you're through at five today. I think that's in ten minutes. I came by because I still intend to take you to dinner. You said you'd go out with me, so you owe me one. Ashley, if I thought you truly didn't like having me around, I'd be gone." He reached out to touch her wrist lightly with his forefinger with feathery strokes that sent tingles radiating through her. "Actually," he said, his voice dropping and getting the husky note that made her sizzle, "I'm looking for the woman who spent the weekend with me."

"I think I lost my mind that weekend."

"Let's talk about it during dinner." He glanced over her shoulder. "May I see your office?"

As her mind raced for an answer, she hesitated, and he smiled. "Good." He draped his arm across her shoulders. "Show me around and then I'll take you to eat and we can talk."

While her mind wrestled with what she should have said and what she *could* say, she walked with him, but most of her attention was on his arm across her shoulders and his side brushing against hers. She had to get rid of him. He was way too take-charge, and she didn't want him discovering that she was pregnant. She loathed the prospect of pity. She didn't want a dutiful proposal. Even more unwanted would be Ryan making decisions about her and her baby. Most frightening of all, she didn't want him to use his millions to try to take her baby away from her.

From the first moment in the doctor's office, when she had almost fainted at the news, she had wrestled with how to deal with Ryan over the matter.

He had used condoms, but the doctor had told her they weren't a hundred percent foolproof. So on a wild weekend that was a once in a lifetime fling for her, she had gotten pregnant by a man she barely knew. As she walked beside him, she rubbed her forehead. How complicated her life had become!

Ashley hadn't figured out yet how to break the news to her father, her brother and her grandmother, let alone Ryan.

She had considered every aspect, and finally had decided that the best possible thing that could happen would be to keep Ryan out of her life until after the baby was born.

She had no idea what his reaction to her pregnancy would be. She knew the day would come when she would have to let him know that he had fathered a child. But she wanted it far in the future, when she had her baby in her arms and her life established, with Ryan Warner far out of it and happily involved with another woman. The last part still hurt to think about, but Ashley knew it was the wisest course.

"This is nice, Ashley," he said as they approached her front door, with its fan transom gracing the top and long, low redwood boxes of blooming flowers on either side. "I've forgotten what you told me. How long have you been a wedding planner?"

"Almost a year," she answered, barely thinking about the question.

He reached out to open her door for her, letting her enter ahead of him. Carlotta was gazing at Ryan with a smile and obvious curiosity.

"Hi," she said.

"Carlotta, this is Ryan Warner. Ryan, this is my receptionist and secretary, Carlotta Reyna," Ashley said, while Carlotta reached out to shake his hand.

Ashley took his arm. "I'm going to show Ryan the office. I'll close up tonight," she told her employee, who nodded, barely able to take her eyes from Ryan.

"You do have an effect on women," Ashley said when they'd crossed the hall, out of earshot. "I thought Carlotta was going to faint with pleasure when you shook her hand."

He grinned and shrugged. "I'm not having the effect where it's important," he replied.

She inhaled. "I walked into that one. You'll probably get the same reaction from my assistant. Both are single."

"I have only one interest."

Ignoring his answer, even though it made her breath catch, Ashley led him into a large room in the front and waved her hand toward the shelves of oversize books. "This space is for clients. I have a lot of materials in here to give them choices about cakes and decorations."

Ryan looked around the cheerful space with its tables and comfortable-looking chairs, and she wondered if he was even remotely interested in her business.

"Introduce me to your assistant and show me your office," he said, studying Ashley with a hungry look.

As she gazed at his handsome features, she thought, *If only.* Immediately, she stopped that train of thought. There were no if onlys. She had to get Ryan out of her office and her life. "Come with me," she said briskly. She knew he was right behind her as she entered the hall, and then he fell into step beside her.

She almost collided with Jenna, who saw Ryan and smiled.

"Jenna, this is Ryan Warner. Ryan, meet my assistant, Jenna Fremont."

"You're really Ryan Warner," Jenna said, sounding as if she were meeting a movie star.

"I'm the one and only. And you're really Jenna Fremont," he said, teasing her and grinning.

She looked as if she would melt as she smiled up at him. "I'm the only Jenna around here." She giggled. "It's great to meet you. I've seen your pictures all over."

"Not on Most Wanted posters, I hope," he kidded, eliciting more giggles.

"I'm showing Ryan our offices. I'll lock up, Jenna."

"It was nice to meet you, Jenna," he said. "I'll see you again, I'm sure."

"Oh, I hope so," she cooed, and Ashley prayed that she'd never be that impressed with any man herself.

"They obviously think you're awesome. If not Carlotta, why don't you take Jenna to dinner?" Ashley suggested, when they were alone.

He smiled.

"She doesn't get my heart pounding, either," he said. "It's interesting how you want to hand me off to someone else."

Ignoring his comment, she motioned toward an open door. "Here's my office."

Like a cat in new surroundings, he circled the spacious room, looking at pictures on the wall and at a table that held a spread of wedding snapshots. At her desk, he paused and leaned over, and she wondered what he was looking at. Her calendar, she realized.

"Ah, you're free tonight. Good."

She shook her head, knowing she had already lost the argument.

"I promise, we'll have a great evening," he said, his gaze boring into her, and she could feel the sparks dancing between them. Attraction was hot and all but crackled in the air. At the same time, there was a clash of wills.

"I'll take you to your favorite place, unless you'd rather

go to mine," he said, giving her another one of those knee-melting smiles that made her remember being in his arms. As if the issue were settled, he moved on, looking at books and pictures on her shelves, picking up an old snapshot of her on the farm with her dad.

Holding the frame in his well-shaped hand, Ryan studied the picture and then glanced at her. "Nice, Ashley. Do you miss the farm?"

"No. I don't want to farm. My brother can do that with my dad."

Ryan glanced at his watch. "It's after five, so that means we can close now. I'll drive, and bring you back later to get your car."

"Ryan, we're not—"

He narrowed the space between them and slipped his arms around her waist. "I want to be with you, talk to you and see you again," he said in a hoarse voice. He trailed one hand up to stroke her nape lightly, evoking tingles. "Get your purse and I'll help you lock up."

He was gone from her private office, his long legs carrying him in an easy stride into the hallway. She shook her head and stepped into her small adjoining bathroom to look at herself in the mirror. "Get rid of him," she whispered. Why did he have to be so damnably handsome? And sexy and fascinating. Why did she respond so to him? she wondered, and then remembered the reactions of Jenna and Carlotta. What female didn't respond to him?

Squaring her shoulders, Ashley took a deep breath and left the room, switching off the lights and going to lock up.

He was standing beside the alarm control box. "Do you have a code for this?" he asked.

She told him, then watched while he punched buttons.

"You did it all correctly," she said as they left. "You're efficient."

"Thank you," he replied. "I'm glad to hear I have some pluses."

"You have too many pluses," she remarked dryly, and received a curious stare from him.

"That's interesting. Too many," he repeated. "Does this mean you want some uncivilized behavior from me?"

"Hardly," she muttered.

"Don't I wish!" he replied. He glanced around. "This is a good location for you, isn't it? Just the right ambience, and probably caters to an upscale group of clients most of the time."

She nodded, thinking that she could add observant to his admirable qualities. As she walked beside him to his car, he slowed his stride to hers and continued to talk about businesses around them, noticing several that tied in to her own.

He held open the door to the black sports car. When he went around to get in, she ran her hand over the elegant leather seat, reminded again of the differences in their worlds. As soon as he was seated beside her, he turned to look at her. "Do you have a favorite restaurant?"

She shrugged. "I'll let you pick where we go. What's your favorite, Ryan?"

"Do you like steak, lobster or pheasant?"

"I like most everything if it isn't too spicy," she replied.

"Including tall, black-haired businessmen?"

"You have to flirt, don't you?"

"With you, absolutely. All right, I'll take you to one of my favorite spots," he said, smiling at her. He ran his finger along her cheek. "I really missed you," he said in a thick voice that affected her as much as his light touches.

"I find that hard to believe," she replied dryly, glad he couldn't detect her racing heartbeat at that moment.

"I'll admit that I haven't been sitting home staring at the wall," he said, giving her another disarming smile, "because I didn't know whether I'd ever see you again or not."

"Actually, Saturday was a surprise."

"I hope one you liked. I'm working on changing your standoffish attitude."

She couldn't keep from smiling at him.

While they talked, he drove swiftly through the traffic. At the restaurant's canopy-covered entrance, a uniformed valet came to hold open her door.

The dining area opened onto a large deck built over a pond covered with blooming water lilies. Strings of colored lanterns hung above the tables, and bright yellow and red bougainvillea spilled from hanging pots.

They were led to a linen-covered table overlooking the pond. Seated facing Ryan, Ashley knew she would remember this place and evening forever. Their waiter handed her a thick black menu, then gave Ryan a wine list and made suggestions.

"If you like lobster, it's very good here. The steaks are excellent, too," Ryan said, offering her the wine list.

Smiling, she shook her head. "I'll just have a glass of ice water."

Ryan ordered white wine for himself, and when they were alone, he reached across the table to take her hand. His grip was strong and his fingers warm. The slight contact was disturbing and heightened her longing.

"There has to be a reason you don't want to see me again. And there has to be more to it than you just lost your head that weekend. I thought we were having a grand time."

"Ryan, try to understand. That weekend was so contrary to my nature."

"That's fine, but now we know each other. If you want to back off and take things slowly, we can. If we just met and I asked you out, would you go?"

"Yes, I probably would, but this is different. We have a history, and you want what we had that weekend, while I don't."

"I just said we can take renewing our relationship slowly," he said, holding her hand and rubbing her knuckles lightly with his thumb.

"Ryan!"

A woman's voice cut across their conversation and Ryan released Ashley's hand as he stood. "Hi, Kayla," he said. "Ashley, this is Kayla Landon. Kayla, meet Ashley Smith."

Ashley smiled at a statuesque redhead who should have been able to make Ryan forget all about seeing anyone else. She was dressed in a figure-hugging black dress that had spaghetti straps and ended well above her knees. Ashley recognized the woman as the one who had been talking to Ryan at his condo that Sunday morning.

"How do you do," Ashley said, and received a frosty look and a nod before Kayla turned to Ryan.

"You'll get my message when you get to your condo," she told him. "I hope to see you Saturday night at my party. The last one was such fun," she purred, placing her hand on his arm.

"I'll give you a call, Kayla," he said casually.

"Make it tomorrow." She brushed his cheek with a kiss, turning to walk away without saying anything to Ashley.

"Now, where were we?" Ryan asked, sitting and facing Ashley.

"She's the woman who was in your condo that Sunday I was there."

"Ah," he said, studying her. "That's why you disappeared without a word."

"Not altogether. It just reminded me of the differences between us," she said. "You and I reside in separate worlds. You have your wealth and ritzy lifestyle. I grew up on a farm and have worked in the city less than a year. I practically have hay in my hair."

He smiled and reached over to twirl a long blond strand around his thumb. "I'll comb my fingers through your hair later and see if I can find any hay," he said in his rich, magnetic voice.

She drew a deep breath. "You're making this a trying problem."

"I'm not the one being difficult. To me, the situation is simplicity itself. Man wants to go out with woman. Man and woman have fabulous time together. What's troublesome about that?"

"You go too fast," she replied. "I regret that weekend, but I can't take it back and undo it."

"All right, we'll go slow. The weekend never happened. We just met at the wedding last Saturday, I want to see you and you're here to eat dinner with me. This is good. Simple." He reached across the table again and laced his fingers with hers. "And in the interest of having a great evening, let's put this discussion on hold until later."

"That is just your way of ending the argument," she said and received another disarming smile.

"And as far as being from different worlds, do you know where and how I grew up?"

"No, we never got around to talking much that weekend we were together," she said, and he smiled.

"You brought up the weekend. I didn't," he pointed out. "My dad did whatever he could find to do—dishwasher, served food in cafeterias, ditchdigger. My mom cleaned houses. We had almost nothing. I'd wager that, growing up, you had a more comfortable life than I did."

"I wasn't aware of your history. I knew you were self-made, because that's in news stories, but not much else. Except the beautiful, sophisticated women you see."

He gave a dismissive wave of his hand. "That's tabloids looking for something sensational. My history is simple. My mom died too young. Dad's still living, and my brothers and I take care of him. He's worked hard all his life and he doesn't need to now. I'm the oldest. I helped my two brothers get started, and they're doing well. Brett is a commercial pilot and Cal, my youngest brother, is an accountant who works for me. I started earning money mowing lawns when I was eleven years old."

Ashley nodded, realizing their worlds were not as far apart as she had thought. Yet she had a difficult time imagining him living in poverty. "So how did you make this miraculous climb to millionaire status?" she asked.

"Long story. Some luck, hard work and help from friends. Nick Colton and Jake Thorne were buds, and both came from simple beginnings, as I did. We made a pact in college to reach millionaire status and to help each other get there."

"Wow! That's impressive," she said. "All of you succeeded."

"Yeah, Nick most of all. They're great friends to have. We all played football in high school and college, and worked for a landscape outfit during summers. We started doing that after our sophomore year in high school. We were all tall. I played pro ball for two years and invested every dime with Jake, who was a whiz in finance from the start. Then I quit football to build hotels."

"No wonder the three of you are such close friends."

"I couldn't have made it without both of them." Ryan paused when their waiter returned with tossed salads on crystal plates and a loaf of golden bread. "How often do you go home to the farm?" he asked, when the waiter departed.

"Since moving here, I've been busy with weddings on weekends, so it's really been difficult to get there. I've gone home for holidays, and I went in February for a weekend because my assistant handled the weddings."

The waiter appeared with their entrees. Ashley glanced down at her plate of shrimp, covered with sun-dried tomatoes and sliced mushrooms and resting on angel hair pasta, while Ryan's plate held a juicy, thick sirloin.

After the first bite, she smiled. "This is fantastic, Ryan. No wonder this restaurant is what you like best."

"No. This is a favorite eating place. I have something else I like best," he said in a deep voice, his green eyes intense on her. She knew he was flirting. "I think I've become a challenge to you. Maybe if I start hanging on each word and looking at you in an adoring manner the way Carlotta and Jenna do, you'll run for the hills."

"Try it and see," he said with a twinkle in his eyes.

She couldn't resist taking his hand and batting her eyes. "Oh, Ryan, tell me more about yourself," she drawled, leaning forward and speaking in a breathless voice.

He inhaled and the amusement vanished from his expression. "That just makes me want to get the check so we can leave and I can be alone with you," he growled. "I can lose interest in food and dinner conversation."

Straightening, she yanked her hand away. "That didn't have the effect I expected. I won't try that one again," she announced, and once more he smiled, but his gaze was speculative.

"I blew that in a hurry," he said. "I have to tell you, that's been the best moment of the night so far. Sure you don't want to continue?"

"Don't get your hopes up, because it won't happen."

"I should've acted indifferent, but that's absolutely impossible with you. Okay, if we have to start over, why don't you tell me about yourself. What's in your future? What do you want out of life? I don't believe we discussed that before."

His question brought her situation crashing back, and the fun she'd been having with him changed as she remembered she intended to discourage and get rid of him. She shrugged. "I like my job and hope to continue it. Since it's a franchise, it's almost like my own business. I get a cut of the profits, so if business increases, my income grows."

"That's good," he said, nodding. "Working for yourself, if it's successful, is satisfying."

"On your level it certainly would be," she remarked dryly.

"On yours, too. You just said so. So what's the best wedding you've done?"

"The one I enjoyed the most…" She paused to think a moment. "Probably one last December. It was a Christmas wedding, with reds and greens and beautiful decorations," she said, telling him about the ceremony and wondering if he was really interested, their conversation drifting to other topics as they enjoyed their time together.

Her shrimp was delicious, but she didn't have much of an appetite, and she noticed that neither did Ryan. While she talked, he listened, studying her and holding her hand. Each volatile contact heightened her awareness of him.

They discussed various subjects, and Ryan occasionally flirted, until he finally motioned to the waiter for their check.

When she looked around, she saw they were almost the last customers. She glanced at her watch. "My word, it's ten o'clock. We've been here for hours."

"Actually, not for hours. Time flies when you're having fun," he quipped as he smiled at her. "And I have had a great time tonight."

While wind tangled locks of his black hair, lights in the parking lot threw his cheeks into shadows, highlighting his prominent cheekbones. She admired his self-assurance and optimism. He was confident, handsome and good company, making her wish that the situation were different between them. She blamed herself that it wasn't, and again tried to pay attention to their conversation.

"You know I've had a great time, too," she said. "And I know you want me to admit it."

"Damn straight. Your confession reassures me," he said, looking at her.

"As if you need encouragement," she said, laughing when they reached his car. With a smile, he swung open the door.

"Are you saying I'm arrogant?"

"You're confident. How's that?"

"Much better. I'll settle for confident." He leaned closer to talk to her as she settled inside. Then he shut the door, and she watched him stride around the car and slide in beside her.

"Your place or mine?" he asked.

"My place and—"

"Don't make hasty decisions," he urged. "Let's see. I told you I'd go slowly and I have. Isn't that right?"

"Yes, it is," she had to answer, because he had been. But that didn't mean he would continue to, and she knew every minute they were together forged a stronger bond between them.

"Tell me where you live. And I'll come get you in the morning and take you to work since you left your car at the office."

"Well, there's no point in arguing this one with you," she said, telling him her address.

She gave him the combination to get through the wrought iron gates of her apartment complex and they drove past several blocks of single-story redbrick duplexes until she directed him to hers. He got out to open her door, and walked her to the front porch, where she faced him.

"It's been a super evening, Ryan."

"It's early, really early," he said. "I'd like to see your place."

Part of her wanted him to come inside, and another part wanted to tell him to go. He stood in silence, waiting patiently, and she couldn't resist. "Do you want to come in?" she asked with a smile, already knowing that was exactly what he hoped to do.

"Thanks, and of course."

She opened her door and stopped to switch off the alarm system and turn on the light in the short entryway.

Ryan entered and she led him into the living room, turning on a lamp while, he looked around. "It's great, Ashley," he said.

"I moved here about a month ago, and I'm just getting new furniture," she explained, trying to view it from his eyes. An Impressionist print in a gilt frame hung above an oak mantel above the brick fireplace. Her sofa and matching wing chair were upholstered in blue antique velvet, and she had a polished hardwood floor, but her place was modest and small compared to his sprawling high-rise condo with its terrace and magnificent view of Dallas.

He had four bedrooms, an entertainment center, an exercise room, a living area and dining room, all filled with elegant fruitwood furniture, and every convenience. Her duplex had to be unimpressive to him, but he was being polite.

"In here is the living area, where I spend all my time," she said, leading him into a small, less formal room with a sofa upholstered in bright flowers and two matching chairs. An oak coffee table sat in front of the sofa.

He walked over to a wooden game table in one corner of the room to look at the chess set on it. "Ah, a game in progress."

"I'm playing with someone via the computer," she said.

"We'll have to have a game," he said. "We won't disturb this one, but sometime soon, or when you finish this one, we can play."

"I imagine you're excellent at chess," she said, unable to picture him doing anything that he didn't consistently manage to succeed at.

"We'll see," he said. "It's difficult to judge yourself."

She laughed. "No, it isn't! You just don't want to admit, especially before we've played, that you rarely lose."

"I'm going to have to improve my image with you," he teased.

"No, and don't even try," she replied, realizing she was giving him one challenge after another.

Bookshelves lined one wall, and Ryan strolled across the room to study the contents of her shelves. Ashley knew she was going to remember him prowling around her duplex. She looked at his broad shoulders and recalled with absolute clarity how he'd look nude, walking away from the bed.

Drawing a deep breath, she tried to focus her mind elsewhere, talking without half thinking about what she was saying. "My kitchen is over here," she said, leading him into a space that was about one-sixth the size of his. It had a small eating area and a tiny island in the center. "And that's it." She smiled at him. "Unless you want to see my utility room."

"I haven't seen your bedroom," he reminded her. "Give me the deluxe tour."

"Sure," she replied, trying to sound casual and not think about a bed and Ryan in it.

"Here it is," she said, and he followed her into her blue bedroom, walking around to look at items on her desk, pictures on the wall and memorabilia on her shelves. He reached out to pick up one of her tennis trophies. "You're good at tennis. We'll have to play."

"Right now I've given it up," she said, and watched his dark eyebrows arch.

"How come?" he asked, replacing the trophy on the shelf.

She realized she couldn't give him the right answer and tried to think of an excuse. But silence stretched, and she began to panic, searching for something to say.

"Tennis elbow," she answered at last.

"Too bad. I was looking forward to a match with you. Chess and tennis. There are two things we both enjoy, so we might as well do them together when we can."

"They're both competitive."

"All the better," he said softly. "I like competing with you."

"I suspect you're happy to compete with the world because most of the time, you're satisfied with the outcome," she said, and he smiled.

"What do you do for your elbow?" he asked, walking over to her.

"There's not much I can do," she replied, avoiding his eyes and wishing she could think of another subject. "Now you've seen my room."

He turned to look at her bed. "I'll know where to picture you in my mind when I talk to you on the phone." His voice had lowered a notch, and she wondered if he was remembering their weekend together, too.

"That's the tour. There's an extra bedroom. Want something to drink?"

"Sure. I'll have pop."

He strolled beside her as they returned to the kitchen, where she got pop for him, ice water for herself and a plate of cookies. "We can go in the living room where it's more comfortable," she said. Seconds later, she was sitting on the sofa. He chose one of the chairs, putting distance between them, and she realized he was doing what he'd promised—going slowly.

"Has your family seen this place?"

She shook her head. "Not yet. My dad and brother don't get into the city often unless there's a cattle sale or something like that. My grandmother hardly ever leaves our area."

"How's your dad feeling?"

"He's getting along all right from what my brother tells me. Jeff says Dad is still working too hard for a man who's had a heart attack, but there's nothing any of us can do about that. The flood last year was another big blow. Health insurance is an endless problem."

"And you're still helping out financially?" Ryan asked bluntly, and she nodded.

"Yes, I'm happy to," she replied.

"I know what you mean," he said, and she wondered if Ryan even remembered the sacrifices of his early years.

He stretched out his long legs. "I'm sorry your family has problems."

"We'll get through them. Dad says we always have."

"So what weddings are coming up?" Ryan asked,

changing the subject. As she talked, she realized he was a good listener.

Finally, he stood and picked up his glass. "I'll put this in the kitchen and then I better go. It's late."

She glanced at her watch and was surprised to see it was nearly one in the morning. "Great heavens! On work nights I go to bed early."

"Sorry if I kept you up past your bedtime. You should've thrown me out."

"Oh, sure," she said. "Leave your glass. I'll put it up."

He crossed the room to her. "Since I'm taking you to work in the morning, eat breakfast with me tomorrow. That's harmless."

"Ryan, nothing is 'harmless' with you," she answered.

"Ah, now that's great news," he replied, and she shook her head. "So even breakfast with me is different from breakfast with John Doe or Susie Smith? Sometime I'll try to discover why, but not yet. Tonight, I'm taking it ever so slowly—don't you agree?"

"Of course, and you have to hear me say that, too."

"I just want to make certain I'm doing what you like," he said with great innocence. He stood inches away, and was bantering her, but she had spent an enjoyable evening with him. They had touched lightly and casually, but each contact was fiery, and longing had steadily built, until now she ached to wrap her arms around him and kiss him. She had no intention of doing so, yet she was certain that before he told her goodbye, that was exactly what he would do. She couldn't imagine he would walk away without a kiss.

"I'll pick you up, so let's have breakfast."

"All right," she said, glancing at her watch. "I have to have my sleep. I'll call and arrange to go in late, so can you come at half-past eight—or does that make you too late?"

"Half-past eight it is." They walked to the door, and he turned to face her.

"Thanks for the delicious dinner," she said. "It was a nice evening."

"I thought it was fantastic. I can't wait until breakfast. Night, Ashley," he said.

"Good night, Ryan," she replied, while her heart raced. To her surprise, he turned and strolled toward his car. She was amazed he hadn't given her even a light kiss, and she tried to ignore the ripple of disappointment she felt.

She waved to him and went inside, locking up and switching off lights. She was getting more involved with him instead of less, she knew, and wondered how much that was going to complicate her life.

It wasn't until she showered for work the next morning that she realized she had made a big mistake.

Worrying, she blew her hair dry, her thoughts on Ryan. She had promised to eat breakfast with him, forgetting completely that all too often she suffered morning sickness.

She knew she could never get him to cancel coming to fetch her. She didn't have a car, since she'd left it at work to go to dinner with him. Mulling over what to do, she dressed in a navy skirt and white blouse, then looped and pinned her hair on her head.

Promptly at half-past eight, Ryan arrived and rang her doorbell. When she opened it, she lost her breath at the sight of him.

Dressed in a charcoal suit and red tie, he looked incredibly handsome. "My, you look great," she couldn't resist saying, reminded again that her baby would have the most handsome father possible.

"That's my line," he said, his warm gaze traveling

slowly over her. He inhaled and his chest expanded. When his eyes met hers again, she drew a long breath, because she could see desire in the depths of green.

"Let me get my purse," she said, realizing her voice was breathless and wondering if he noticed.

As she returned, he watched her. She felt self-conscious, tingly, but couldn't resist hoping she enticed him.

"You're gorgeous," he said quietly.

"Thanks, even though it's a bit of an exaggeration. White blouse, navy skirt, ordinary office clothes," she said, waving her hand toward herself.

"Not to me. And I'm seeing you without them. I still have a memory."

Her pulse skipped. "Forget it, Ryan," she said. "You go out and I'll set my alarm," she added.

"You've already triggered mine," he drawled, with a sexy innuendo that made her breath catch.

As he drove, she tried to keep the conversation light, maintaining a stream of topics so they wouldn't get into anything personal.

The sun was bright, the air clear and the sky a deep blue. The beautiful spring day lifted her spirits, and she wondered how much of her bubbling enthusiasm was because of the glorious day and how much was due to the charmer seated beside her.

He took her to an expensive restaurant where she had never eaten. The glassed-in dining area held an abundance of hanging green plants and pots of tropical flowers, all giving an open-air feeling and adding to the springtime ambience.

His eyebrows arched when she ordered only milk and an English muffin.

"I'm not particularly hungry," she explained, already too aware of smells of coffee and bacon wafting in the air. She wished she had never accepted the invitation to breakfast with him, but she was into it now, and she tried to avoid thinking about food or looking at any that went by, carried by waiters.

When her muffin and milk were placed in front of her, she didn't really want them.

Worse, Ryan was served a platter holding an omelet and slices of bacon, patties of sausage and fat, golden biscuits. He had steaming coffee and a chilled glass of orange juice.

Her queasy stomach churned, and she excused herself, rushing to the ladies' room because of nausea. To her relief, it was an elegant restaurant and the ladies' room had a sofa. Stretching out, she laid folded paper towels soaked in cold water on her forehead, thankful Ryan couldn't see her.

A few minutes later, a waitress came in and spotted her. She asked if Ashley was okay.

"Yes, thanks," she replied, smiling. "I just felt faint." To her relief, the waitress nodded and left.

Ashley stayed until she felt she could join Ryan again. With her stomach still churning, she returned. Coming to his feet as she approached the table, he reached out to take her arm. "Let's go. I've already taken care of the check," he said, holding her arm.

"You're having to leave your breakfast behind," she said, wanting to get to the sanctuary of her office, and barely thinking about what she was saying.

"That's no problem. Ashley, I'm taking you to my doctor."

"No, you're not!" she declared emphatically. "I'm fine."

When he lapsed into an uncustomary silence, she wondered if she had been too abrupt. She slid into his car and shut her eyes, resting her head against the seat. She straightened when she heard him opening his door, and glanced up to find him studying her intently.

Her heart thudded. "It's just a minor upset, Ryan. Really it is. Don't worry, and take me to my office."

She knew she should force some kind of cheerful banter and get his mind off the incident, but she was wrung out. The motion of the car wasn't helping, and she was desperate to escape.

At her office, he came around the car to take her arm again. "I'm fine. I promise," she repeated.

"I'll go inside with you," he insisted.

She didn't feel like arguing, and he would soon be gone. She walked in silence with him and was relieved they didn't encounter Jenna or Carlotta.

In her office she turned to thank Ryan, while he closed the door and turned to face her, standing only a few feet away with his hands on his hips.

Her heart began to drum, because he wasn't leaving as she expected him to.

"Now tell me what's really wrong with you!" he demanded quietly.

Three

Taking her time to answer him, she fiddled with her watch, while his curiosity grew.

He could remember that fabulous weekend with her and the sizable breakfasts they'd had each morning, without any unpleasant upsets on her part. He thought about her easy, slow walk that indicated time wasn't a ruling factor in her character—something so removed from his driven life that he had been intrigued. Usually smiling, relaxed, taking time to savor life, people and her surroundings, she'd interested him from the first moment he'd met her. Now, as she fidgeted and remained silent, his questions increased.

She had been sick in the restaurant. He'd had a waitress check on her and was told that Ashley said she was fine, but was lying on the sofa with wet towels on her forehead.

He could also recall how she'd had wine with her

dinners their first weekend. Now she was drinking ice water. Everything added up to a change.

"Ashley, what is it?" he prompted.

"I'm all right," she said without looking at him. Circling her desk, she sat and bent down to open a drawer.

Right now, she was deathly pale, and he was afraid she would pass out in front of him. He liked her, wanted to know her better, and the weekend they'd spent together had been the most fabulous, passionate time of his life. He hadn't been able to forget her or get her out of his thoughts, and he was concerned now.

Grabbing a chair, he circled the desk and sat close beside her. "Tell me the truth, Ashley. You know what's wrong. You're a lousy liar."

She looked at her fingers laced together in her lap. "Leave me be, Ryan. I mean it," she said forcefully, and raised her head.

Surprised, he was taken aback by the fire in her eyes. Bright spots of color stained her otherwise pale cheeks.

His gaze searched hers. "All right, I'll leave," he said. Halfway to the door, he stopped and looked at her. "Can I do anything? Get you something?"

"No, but thank you," she answered flatly. "Just let me be."

As he headed out of the room and reached for the knob, he wondered whether she was sick every morning. He'd started to leave when it dawned on him. Morning sickness.

He already had the door open and he closed it. No wine. No tennis. She wanted him out of her life. *Morning sickness.* He turned to look at her, examining her closely. She looked the same as ever. Her waist was tiny, her stomach flat.

She blinked and glowered at him. "Just get out of here, Ryan."

"How long has this been happening?"

Color flushed her cheeks again. "Not long. I don't know. I'm all right."

He stared at her, thinking it was impossible, but knowing it wasn't. "You're pregnant," he declared.

When she flinched, he knew he was right.

Clenching her fists, she raised her chin. "It doesn't concern you."

He was shaken and wondered who she'd been with. "How far along are you?"

"A couple of months," she replied. "I haven't told my family or anyone yet, so I would appreciate it if you don't."

"Don't worry," he snapped. "Who's the man?"

"I'm not giving out his identity," she replied stiffly, but there was a flash in her eyes that shook him. He walked closer to her.

"How far along are you?" he asked again. "Tell me the truth, Ashley." He placed his hands on her shoulders. "How many months are you? Dammit, I want to know."

"Get out. I'm not telling you."

"You know I can find out some way. I have enough money to get the information I want."

Suddenly she looked frightened, and gazed wide-eyed at him while shock buffeted him. "How many months?" he said, barely able to get out the words.

"Over three," she said, glaring at him. "This is my baby and I don't want any interference. Now, you get out of here."

Stunned, he stared at her. "There isn't another man, is there?" he asked.

"Get out, Ryan."

He knew the answer. He was the father of Ashley's baby. Shocked, he couldn't believe it, but he could tell from looking at her that it was true. "We used protection."

"Get out of my office!" she snapped.

Stunned by the news, he turned and left, going out to the car to sit behind the wheel and try to absorb what he'd learned. He started it up and drove a block, then pulled to the curb, cutting the engine to stare into space. He was the father of Ashley's baby! She was pregnant from their weekend together. He had difficulty accepting the truth. He'd used condoms, and nothing had failed, that he had known. He was stiff with shock, unaware of the traffic pouring past him, of the spring morning, of joggers running by.

Ashley was going to have a baby. *His* baby.

Shaking, Ashley walked around her desk and sank into the chair, calling Carlotta on the intercom to tell her that if Ryan Warner appeared, she was not available to see him. Then she closed her eyes.

What a mess she'd made of the morning! And exactly what she'd hoped to avoid had happened. Ryan knew the truth.

He'd been shocked, and obviously didn't want any part of it—that much was a relief to her, even though at the same time, it angered her. She knew she shouldn't feel conflicted about his reaction, but she did.

She rubbed her throbbing forehead and longed to undo the morning. Wished she had been wise enough last night to refuse to eat breakfast with him today.

When her intercom buzzed, she groaned. She didn't feel like dealing with anyone yet. She pushed the button to speak to Carlotta.

"Ryan Warner is on his way to your office. I'm sorry, I couldn't stop him."

"That's all right," Ashley said, knowing her receptionist couldn't have kept out a determined male like him.

Before she could answer his knock, he strode into her office, closing the door behind him.

"I don't want to see you, but I don't suppose that matters to you," she said.

"No, it doesn't. You weren't going to tell me about my baby." He flung the accusation at her in a low, steely tone.

"Yes, I was, but not until after the baby is born, because I don't want your interference."

"How about my help?"

"I don't want that, either," she said.

He crossed the room and sat in the chair he'd placed beside hers earlier, gazing intently at her. "Why the hell not?" he asked. A muscle worked in his jaw.

"You'll take charge of my life. I want to take care of myself," she stated in a haughty voice, and raised her chin.

"It seems to me you sure as hell could use some financial help. You should welcome it."

"I know what I'm doing."

"And it seems to me you should let your family know."

"I'll tell them soon. Other than the doctor, you're the first to hear about it. Look, your immediate reaction was an honest one—you tore out of here in shock and didn't want any part of this. Don't try to include yourself now out of a sense of guilt."

"I left in shock and because you kept asking me to go. I'm not suffering any guilt," he insisted.

"Oh, please," she said, giving him a skeptical look. She was annoyed with him, certain he must be steeped in guilt, to return as he had with an offer of help. His tie was awry, his hair tangled on his forehead and he looked as if he had been wrestling with something difficult. She waved her hand. "Go on, Ryan. I'll keep you posted."

"No," he said. "I can easily help out, and this is my

baby, too. I can provide a nanny, and you'll have to have a nursery."

"See, this is exactly why I didn't want you involved!" she exclaimed in exasperation. "You're making my decisions." She rubbed her forehead. "I don't feel well. Why don't you leave me alone this morning and we'll talk later. I need some peace and quiet."

Looking frustrated, he stood with clenched fists. "I'll see you tonight. I'll bring steaks and come to your place. We need to talk about this."

"Whether I want to or not," she said.

"Damn straight! This is a life-changing event and I'm involved in it whether you like it or not. You can't say no to me when it's my baby." He strode out of the office and slammed the door behind him.

She ran to yank open the door. "Then eat before you come. I won't feel like eating, anyway!"

He turned around and with long steps came back. "You need to eat dinner."

"I know that," she replied in exasperation. "I'll eat before you come. You do the same."

He nodded. "See you around seven." He hurried out the front and she returned to her office, closing her door and going to sit behind her desk.

She stared into space and wished she had done far more to get him out of her life and keep him from discovering the truth. Now there was no getting rid of him. Ryan was in her life to stay, probably until their baby was grown. *Their baby*. It shocked her to think about her baby in that way, because after discovering her pregnancy, she had closed Ryan out of any connection to the baby until this morning.

An hour later she felt better. She spent the day trying to keep from worrying about Ryan. She left work early to get ready to see him. He was coming over at seven, and she suspected the night would be one of continual clashes.

After eating a small dinner of a poached egg and toast, she bathed and dressed with care. In spite of all her worries and anger with him, excitement bubbled in her at the thought of seeing Ryan.

As she dried her hair, her intercom buzzed. A florist wanted to get through the gate to deliver flowers. When she went to the door, a driver climbed out of a panel truck and came up the walk with a crystal vase containing a huge bouquet of daises and yellow tulips. She took the arrangement and carried it inside, where she set it on a table and paused to read the card.

"To the mother of my baby," was scrawled there. "Can't wait to see you." It was signed with Ryan's bold signature.

She shook her head, reminded that he wasn't going away. She looked again at the card. *The mother of my baby...*

She placed the card carefully into the bouquet and carried it into her living area, placing it on the coffee table where he would see it. Then she finished dressing.

She let her long, straight blond hair fall freely over her shoulders. Wearing pale yellow slacks and a yellow-and-white cotton shirt and sandals, she gazed at her reflection, turning to look at her flat stomach.

Promptly at seven she heard his car. With a sigh, she braced herself to deal with him.

When she opened the door, the sight of him worked its unfailing magic. In a navy short-sleeved knit shirt and chinos, Ryan looked refreshed and his usual cheerful self.

"Come in. Would you like something to drink? Beer, water, wine, pop?" she asked as he entered.

"Cold beer would be good," he said, closing the door. "What are you having?"

"Ice water," she answered.

"I'll help," he said, walking beside her. "I know where things are now." Like everything else he had been doing since learning about the pregnancy, his actions caused her both chagrin and amusement, because he took charge as if it were his kitchen. As soon as he handed her the glass of water and got his beer, they went into the family room and she motioned toward the flowers. "These are lovely."

"Not nearly as gorgeous as the recipient," he responded, setting down his beer and taking her ice water to place it on the coffee table. Her heart thudded when he turned to slide his arms around her waist.

"I went slowly last night. I don't see much need to continue that."

Her heartbeat quickened as she rested her hands on his forearms. Desire smoldered in his gaze as he watched her. "I disagree," she replied. "I still want to take some time. We can get to know each other better."

"Do you know how badly I want to hold and kiss you?" he asked in a husky voice, and her opposing emotions tangled fiercely. She needed him to ease up and give her space. At the same time, she ached to throw her arms around him and kiss him.

"Just wait," she said, pushing lightly against his muscled chest. "Give me time here. It's important to me, Ryan," she said, in spite of her yearning to reach for him.

As she looked into his eyes, she wondered if he had any idea what he did to her heartbeat. The longer they stood with locked gazes, the more she wanted him, and the more difficult it was to push away and establish some space between them. His arm tightened around her waist, and what she craved became more important than what she *should* do.

"It's been a long time, Ashley," he whispered as his

gaze dropped to her lips. He leaned down, covering her mouth with his, and his tongue touched hers. Engulfed by longing, she couldn't resist him. She wrapped her arms around his neck as he drew her closer.

While her heart pounded, he leaned over her, kissing her deeply, his tongue stroking hers and building fires in her. The yearning was intense, insistent; her arguments seemed to go up in flames. She yielded to the moment, aware his kisses had comprised all her fantasies and dreams for months now.

In return she poured out her pent-up hunger, which had grown steadily. As he leaned over her, his hand wound in her locks and she tangled her fingers in his thick hair.

His manhood pressed against her. Clinging tightly to him, she moaned. She ached to be rid of the slightest barriers between them, but knew that couldn't happen. Not now. Dimly, she realized she needed to regain control and stop, but not yet. She kissed him wildly, wanting him with all her being. He was exciting and desirable, the man of her dreams, the father of her child.

While they kissed, his hand slipped down her back and over her bottom to cup her against him. His kisses conveyed a desperate hunger, an intense need for her that made her want him even more in return.

He shifted her slightly and his fingers drifted over her breast, his feathery caress electrifying. She moaned again. His touch was a sweet torment that heightened her pleasure.

Finally, she pushed against his chest. When she did, he loosened his hold and she looked up at him. "We have to wait. I'm not ready," she said, her breathlessness denying her words.

"Yes, you are," he replied in a raspy voice. "And I'm more than ready. I've dreamed of you too many nights. I've thought about you more than you can possibly imagine."

His words thrilled her, but she shook her head. "No, I can't. We wait. There's too much complicating our lives."

"This is the best possible time to love each other."

She twisted free and walked away from him, straightening her clothing and trying to get her emotions under control. She turned to face him.

His mouth was red and his expression conveyed his feelings. There was no question he was eager for her.

Fighting the urge to walk into his arms, she stayed where she was. "We need to talk about the future."

"There are other ways to solve this and be happy."

"Lust isn't going to solve anything."

"That isn't how I would describe it. All right, Ashley, we'll make some plans."

"That's exactly what I hoped to avoid. Ryan, I didn't want you to know about the baby this soon because I knew you'd want to take charge. Let me deal with this. It's my life, and you never wanted to become a father."

"This is my baby, too, and you might as well get accustomed to the idea, because I'm not going away." He spoke quietly, but she detected his unyielding tone.

She glared at him. "I want to have this baby and get settled. After that, let's talk about what we'll do."

He crossed the room to take her hand. "This is so simple. Will you marry me?"

While her heartbeat fluttered, she hoped she kept her features impassive. She placed her hand on his cheek. "Your proposal is kind. Thank you, but no."

"Dammit!" he snapped, while fire flashed in his eyes. "I'm not being kind. I'd like to marry you."

"A week ago you wouldn't have considered proposing. This is what you think you're duty bound to do, and it's generous of you. No, I'm sorry, but when I marry, I want it to be with someone I'm wildly in love with, who's just as in love with me. You know we don't have that relationship." She shook her head. "No, Ryan. I knew you would propose, because I know you think you should."

A muscle worked in his jaw and he got a piercing look in his eyes. Ashley braced for whatever he'd say next.

"We're having a baby, which is the best possible reason to wed. Sex between us is fabulous—another dandy reason. Most times we've been out together, we've had a grand time, with the exception of breakfast this morning. We have simple backgrounds, and are in better times now, so we're alike there," he reminded her. While he talked, she had a suspicion he was fighting to maintain patience.

"We're not remotely alike," she retorted. "You're a millionaire. I'm a wedding planner, trying to make ends meet, earn a living to support myself in the city and help my family," she said solemnly. "And that's just a start. There's not one thing you've said that has changed my opinion. We have lust between us and that's no basis to wed. We're having a baby, but a sham marriage won't do anything to make our child's life better. The few times we've been together, we've gotten along, but they're very few and not enough to tell how we'd do in the long haul. A pleasant time over dinner means nothing. We're not getting our lives entangled so you can run things. You're accustomed to control, but that isn't the way this is going to go," she declared, determined to resist him, although a nagging inner voice urged her to accept his offer.

"I don't think you're taking into consideration what would be best for our baby."

She drew a deep breath as she gazed at him. "My baby needs loving parents. I want the man I marry to be my best friend, as well as my lover."

"I qualify on half of that."

"The least important half," she said. "Ryan, as I said, you're a take-charge person and I don't want that. I'm having this baby. I don't want to marry you out of desperation. An unhappy marriage won't be any plus for a baby."

"What makes you think it'll be unhappy?"

"I don't know that it will. But I also don't know that it'll be a solid marriage."

He placed his hands on her shoulders again. "You think about what I can do for our baby. I can give it my name, so it will be a Warner and entitled to Warner money. There'll be more than ample funds for education and travel and nannies. There'll be a father on the scene. You can't just dismiss all that without giving it due thought and consideration."

"I certainly can. At this time, I know I don't want to marry you. In months to come my feelings might change, depending on how our relationship progresses, but marry right now? No way. Give us time, Ryan. Let's just sit, and you tell me about your day, besides what involved the baby and me," she said emphatically.

He stared at her as if she was asking the impossible, but finally he crossed the room to the sofa. Ashley sat on the opposite end, curling her legs beneath her and smiling at him. He sipped his cold beer while she drank ice water, then replaced her glass on the table.

"I want to hear about *your* day. How long have you been having morning sickness?" he asked.

"Almost from the start," she answered, aware of how intently he watched her. She wasn't half as calm as she hoped she looked. To argue with him about doing things for their child had been hard, but she knew she didn't want to move fast and make lifelong decisions on impulse.

"What did the doctor say about it?"

"It should end soon. Actually, he thought it would be over by now."

"And who is the doctor you're seeing?"

She told him, and suspected he was making a mental note to check the man out. "So what did you do today, Ryan?"

"That weekend was awesome, Ashley," he said instead of answering, his words slowing and his tone deepening as he talked. "I can't forget it."

She gazed at him, tingling over what he'd just told her. "It was a great weekend, I'll grant you that," she whispered.

"We can have more like it," he reminded her, and she nodded.

"But not yet, Ryan. I'm not ready yet," she repeated, looking at his handsome features as if memorizing them. "So what about business today? Did it go out the window completely?"

Setting his beer on the table, he scooted closer to her, to touch her shoulder lightly. "As a matter of fact, it did. That's all right. I'll catch up tomorrow. On Thursday, I may have to fly to Chicago, but I'll be here Saturday." He trailed his fingers across her cheek. "So when are you telling your family?"

She looked away, hating the question. "I dread dealing with my family," she confessed. "I think my dad will be hurt."

"If we wed, you won't hurt him. Think about how much easier it would be to inform them."

For just a moment she did consider his offer again, and she was tempted. What a burden that would lift, to announce her marriage to Ryan and then tell her family about the baby. She looked at him and shook her head. "That's the best argument you've presented, but I still say no. I want full command of my life."

"I don't think I'm the only control freak here. You're just as take-charge as I am, and you have a job where you're the authority all the time."

She nodded. "I hadn't ever thought about it, but I suppose you're right. I'm the oldest child in my family, just as you are in yours, and I think it makes a difference. I had to care for my brother a lot of the time."

"I just browbeat mine into doing what I wanted, if they didn't go along in the first place."

She laughed, easing the tension, and they talked about growing up. Yet she had a feeling he was mulling over what he was going to do next. Finally, there was a moment of silence when he leaned away to look at her. He ran his finger along her knee, and she wondered what he was thinking.

"Ashley, I think you and the baby would both be better off if you'd marry me," he said, abruptly changing topics again.

"I don't happen to agree," she retorted, wondering how many times they would argue over their future. She looked at his well-shaped hands, which too often brought memories about him.

"You've said you fear my take-charge ways, but you're just as strong in that department, and I have no doubt you can hold your own with me. I think marriage is definitely in your best interest."

"That's not for you to decide, and we're not getting anywhere arguing about it," she said, impatient with his high-handed determination to get his way.

"No, we're not, so I intend to do something, since I feel marriage is best for all concerned."

Her heart pumped faster while she wondered what he planned, terrified he was going to tell her that he would try to take the baby from her. "Don't do something you'll regret later," she warned.

"I won't," he stated, with so much confidence she braced herself for what was coming. "You marry me, and I'll pay off your family's mortgage, the debts your father has and take care of his insurance. You can't turn down my offer and hurt your family."

Four

Filled with disbelief, she came to her feet. "Ryan Warner, you'll force me into marriage when you know I don't want to marry you. That's despicable!" she exclaimed, glaring at him in fury. Her fists clenched and white-hot anger shot through her.

"Calm down," he ordered quietly, but with a firmness in his voice and a commanding look in his eye that made her take a deep breath and sit down again. "I'm doing exactly that," he assured her. "You have to accept my offer for your family's sake."

Knowing he was right, she stared at Ryan while the implications of his offer both dazzled and angered her.

"I can afford to pay off the mortgage on the farm completely, as well as repair all the damage from the flood. Frankly, your father might want to buy a new place where he won't have to worry about floods, which I'm willing to finance. I can hire some hands to help him, and I can afford to pay for your brother's college education if he wants to go."

"This is blackmail of sorts!" she snapped, taking deep breaths to calm herself.

"I can also see to it that your father has health-insurance coverage. I've got good lawyers who can look into the matter," Ryan continued, speaking as calmly as if he were discussing the weather.

"My family and I don't want charity!" she said tightly.

"It won't be charity," he said patiently, "if we marry. I'll be taking care of things because, if we're married, your family is part of mine and vice versa. I take care of my father, and I'll take care of yours."

"I can't believe you're doing this," she whispered. She shook her head and tears threatened, because she knew she had no choice in the matter.

"You have to accept my proposal and you know it," he said.

Dismayed again, she stared at him. "You want to go into this forced marriage?"

He nodded. "That's exactly what we're going to do. You can save a lot of pain and heartache for you and your family. It should prolong your father's life and give your brother opportunities he would never have otherwise."

Shaking, she gasped for breath. "Damn you and your high-handed ways, Ryan Warner!"

He looked up at her calmly. "Marry me, Ashley, and solve your problems."

"Under conditions like that, what kind of marriage would it be?"

"A damn good one when you get over your anger." He stood to face her, and for the first time, fire flashed in the depths of his green eyes. "This is what's best for you, our baby and your whole family, and you know it."

"If you think I'm going to be filled with gratitude, you're wrong. I'll never forgive you."

"Yes, you will," he replied with that damnable arrogance that increased her fury. He reached down to grasp her shoulders. As she watched him, her heart pounded. The determined gleam in his eyes added to the sparks flying between them. He wrapped his arms around her and lowered his head.

"No!" she exclaimed, her anger growing over his despicable tactics. But his arms tightened, his mouth covered hers, and he kissed her hard.

Standing stiffly in his embrace, she resisted for seconds, but then it was impossible. Demanding and fiery, his kiss conveyed such obvious passion for her that she was shaken. His need stunned her, and the volatile chemistry between them flared.

Overpowered by his kiss, she momentarily forgot her thoughts and arguments. With her heart racing, she wrapped her arms around him and held him tightly, kissing him in return. Never before in her life had she felt that a man wanted her as badly as Ryan did now.

Abruptly, he released her, his arms still wrapped around her waist while he looked down at her. "There! You know what we have is spectacular, and now there's a baby to consider."

With a racing pulse, she struggled to gather her wits. When she did, her anger seethed once again. "Sex is sensational, you mean. And for your information, I *am* considering my baby. You're a dirty fighter," she declared.

"I just intend to win," he answered coolly. "I've made a damn good offer."

She wiggled away and paced across the room to put distance between them. When she turned, he stood with his hands on his hips, his coat pushed open. His whole being conveyed a stubborn determination to get his way. Only the muscle working in his jaw indicated his frayed emotions.

While her fury burned, she felt boxed in, unable to battle him. "I'll think about it."

He shook his head. "No, you decide now. This is something you don't have to think a long time about."

"That's even worse!" she snapped, her rage mushrooming. "It's a monumental, life-changing proposal and you're demanding that I decide right now?"

"We've hashed it over already. We could argue over it for the rest of the year, but we're not going to," he said with absolute certainty.

"You're being ruthless about this!" she protested.

"No, I'm not," he replied with a maddening calm. "I'm being generous and considerate and practical."

"You're no such things! You want this baby and this is your way to get it."

His eyes darkened and a muscle worked in his jaw. "I want what's best for all concerned, and you're not thinking clearly about the matter, so I have to for all three of us."

They faced each other as the silence intensified. She knew he was waiting. Marriage to Ryan... Yet it would save her family... She hadn't allowed herself to consider his offer, which was truly fabulous. Her brother could go to college.

Would her family accept Ryan's charity? She knew they would if he was married into the family. And she knew Ryan could easily afford what he offered.

Rubbing her forehead, she saw there really was no choice. As Ryan stood quietly waiting, she glared at him. "I don't know what kind of marriage you think this will be, when your bride is furious with you!"

He arched one dark eyebrow and continued looking at her, steely eyed.

"All right, Ryan, I'll marry you. But it's not what I want."

"Good," he replied quietly. He crossed the room to her and grasped her upper arms firmly. Her heart pounded and she stared at him. Locks of black hair fell over his forehead and his gaze pierced her. "Ashley, when you get rid of your anger, you'll change. I promise, I'll do everything I can to make you happy."

"Like you have tonight?" she cried bitterly, thinking he was making a meaningless gesture. "You're a bully, Ryan."

"I'll remind you as many times as I have to. I think that I'm doing what's best for all of us," he stated in a tone that was so self-assured she wanted to gnash her teeth. "This is going to help your family tremendously."

Her pulse jumped at the thought. "I'll have to admit that your offer, as far as my family is concerned, is overwhelmingly generous and thrills me. That part will be absolutely wonderful."

"Good," Ryan replied with obvious satisfaction. His hands slid to her shoulders. "Look on the bright side of things."

She shook her head. "Ryan, we'll have an impossible marriage."

He pursed his lips. "If I thought that, I wouldn't persist. I think our marriage is going to be fabulous as soon as you calm down and adjust. And you will."

"You're incredibly arrogant," she told him, looking into those contented green eyes.

"You'll hold your own. I'll pick you up tomorrow night about six and we'll start early for dinner. All right?"

"Why do you even bother to ask?" She rolled her eyes while he gazed at her intently.

"I know you're annoyed with me right now," he said.

"Annoyed!" she exclaimed, deciding he was the most hardheaded man she had ever known. "I'm furious with you, and my rage won't be gone tomorrow night."

"Hopefully, you're wrong," he said. "I'll call one of my lawyers in the morning and get him to start looking into health insurance for your dad. We need to see your family soon to tell them we're engaged, but first we should plan the wedding. "

"You move fast, Ryan."

"Why wait? The sooner I help your father, the better off your family will be." He glanced at his watch. "I'm keeping you up."

She walked with him to the door while her thoughts seethed. He turned to look down at her and his gaze lowered to her mouth, making her pulse drum faster.

"This is good, Ashley," he said quietly, with all the conviction possible. His hands went around her waist and he pulled her to him, lowered his head and kissed her, long and thoroughly. Her resistance was fleeting, gone in seconds. She wrapped her arms around her neck and kissed him back.

Ryan pulled her closer, leaning over her, kissing her until she was moaning with pleasure and thrusting her hips against him. Desire was a hot flame, burning their problems away. She wanted him with a need that shocked her. She ran her hands across his shoulders, tugging free his shirt and sliding one palm over his warm, muscled chest.

When he released her, they were both panting for breath. "We'll stop tonight," he said roughly, and she couldn't interpret the expression in his eyes. She wanted to pull him back into her arms, but she stepped away instead, and in silence watched him go out the door and stride to his car.

When she closed the door behind him, her mind was churning.

Marriage. The idea was staggering. Yet she had to acknowledge, as much as she hated to, that in some ways Ryan was correct. Marriage would solve a lot of her problems.

With her thoughts in a turmoil, she moved sluggishly toward her bedroom. Without realizing what she was doing, she stopped, standing in the middle of the room and staring into space while she mulled over everything that had happened.

Tomorrow night she was having dinner with him, and he intended for them to make wedding plans. She was still in shock over the prospect. The minute Ryan had reappeared in her life, he'd turned it as topsy-turvy as her first encounter with him had been.

She thought again how little they knew each other, and ground her teeth together. She might as well decide what she would wear, she figured—anything to try to keep her mind off what was happening. She knew sleep would be a long time coming.

Trying to collect shards of self-assurance that had been shattered by Ryan's demands, she left work an hour early the next day. She wanted to take her time getting ready, so she would feel and look her best. Even though he hadn't said where they were going for dinner, somewhere casual or dressy, she selected a clinging black dress with a dramatic slashed V-neck trimmed in white that dipped to her waist. The skirt ended above her knees. Her black spiked heels gave her added height.

She swept her hair up on one side and let it fall loosely across her back and down the other side.

Finally she was ready, and while she waited, she thought that Ryan would probably be a great father. And her family would love her baby as much as a child could be loved. For the first time the prospect of telling them excited her. Married to Ryan, she would be able to inform them about the baby with joy and without all the worries she'd had before.

Ryan had been correct about that prediction, and eventually she might admit as much to him. But at the moment, she was so angry with him she didn't care to tell him he'd gotten anything right.

When she heard a car, she glanced at herself in the mirror one last time, seeing a woman who looked poised and dressed for a night out. Uncertainty sent a ripple of worry through her. Had she overdressed? If he'd decided on barbecue and cooking at his place… She put the thought out of mind. With a toss of her head, she picked up her purse and went to the door as the bell rang.

The moment she opened the door, she was reassured about her dress. Ryan wore a dark brown suit and was stunningly handsome. As usual. And she saw the warm approval in his eyes when he looked at her, stepped inside and closed her door behind him.

"You look fantastic!" he said, touching her cheek lightly and then drawing his finger down the edge of the vee of her dress. She inhaled, because his feathery touch stirred hot tingles.

He bent his knees to look into her eyes. "Still angry?" he asked. "Hopefully, I can change that tonight."

"Don't count on it, Ryan," she replied grimly.

He placed his hand on her shoulder. "I hope someday soon you'll forgive me completely."

"We'll see," she said tightly.

He gave her a long, probing look and she wondered what he was thinking. Then he reached for the door.

"I don't need to ask if you're ready to go, so shall we leave?"

She nodded and set her alarm, going out ahead of Ryan. In his sleek, black sports car, she sat far on her side, riding in silence, letting anger smolder and wondering how long he was going to put up with her fury. Or would it wear him down enough that he'd withdraw his offer? She'd soon see.

Then she realized they'd been driving a long time, and she glanced at him with curiosity. "Where are we going?"

"Someplace that I hope is special," he replied easily.

"If you're trying to bribe me into a good humor about this, it won't work," she said, frowning at him.

"Not at all. I want to show you a good time and a night to remember."

"Ryan, how can I possibly forget one moment with you?" she asked in a tight voice.

Then she watched as they swung into the lane for the airport. Her amazement grew when they pulled up to a hangar and crossed the tarmac to a dazzling white jet.

"What are we doing?" she asked, realizing he was completely unpredictable to her.

"I'm just taking you to dinner at a place I hope you like." He took her arm, leading her to the plane while the sun slanted toward the horizon on the warm spring afternoon.

In minutes they were airborne in his private jet. Ashley watched Dallas slip away below, and realized they had banked and were heading south toward the Gulf.

She turned from the window to find Ryan watching her. Her racing heartbeat was one thing that her anger with him hadn't changed. Whenever the magnetic tug of his bedroom eyes focused on her, her pulse accelerated, no matter what she thought about him.

He sat across from her in a plush seat, and the well-decorated, comfortable interior of the plane reminded her of his money everywhere she looked. His money, and she was marrying into it. The idea amazed her, but didn't help her ruffled feelings over his authoritarian manner. She could get along without Ryan and his money. She always had. And she had a family who would love her baby and support her, whether Ryan was on the scene or not.

"Penny for your thoughts," he said.

"I'm still fuming and wondering how you can possibly expect this marriage to work."

"The chances of my marriage to you being happy are vastly greater than the chances for success I figured I had when I was a kid—so much so that this wedding prospect doesn't give me many qualms."

"You have done a complete turnaround since that weekend when you let me know you preferred to remain a bachelor for many years to come."

"I didn't know you then—or had known you only a few hours. I wasn't expecting a baby and I didn't see the great possibilities for the future."

She rolled her eyes and shook her head. "And you expect me to simply turn my life over to you and let you make all the decisions."

"Hardly," he said, smiling at her. He moved to the seat beside her and turned her swivel chair to face him, then cupped her chin in his hand. "Just this one thing. I have to get my way on marriage because it's what's best for all concerned, and I expect the day to come when you'll agree. I don't think we have time to wait and hash it over."

"Yes, we do," she said. "You could take time to court me. We could get to know each other, and then you could propose like a normal person, instead of taking charge and getting your way."

"By offering to end your family's problems? I don't think that's too evil." He was close and his gaze bored into her, making her weak-kneed as she argued with him. When he looked down at her mouth, taunting memories seized her. Her lips parted, tingled, and she couldn't repress her blatant physical response. "Ashley," he whispered, "You're pregnant. Face it, I can make things easier for you."

"It's not evil, Ryan. It's generous and wonderful, but arrogant, and you don't know whether you're getting us into a lasting relationship or not."

"Who knows that for certain when they marry?" he asked, but she focused on his mouth and couldn't think about his question.

"I'd like you in my arms and in my bed," he said. "I want to love you and I don't intend to wait." He touched her cheek lightly. "You have no idea what you do to me."

Her heart thudded at the last and she couldn't get her breath. She ached to reach for him, yet knew this wasn't the time nor place.

"You're a handsome charmer who weaves spells," she accused. "I'm caught in one and don't like it."

"Stop fighting me. Stop resisting both of us. You feel some of what I do. I can see it in your eyes and hear it in your voice and feel it in your throbbing veins."

She turned away. "That has little to do with what I *want*," she said.

She saw him study her. "Did you go to work today?"

"Yes, I did," she replied stiffly.

"That surprises me. I thought you might stay home."

"I left the office early," she said coolly. "And I didn't share my plans with anyone."

"Did you leave ahead of time to get ready for tonight, or because you couldn't work for thinking about our marriage?"

"If you must know, I couldn't work. It was not to get ready for a big evening out with you," she lied.

He fanned himself with his hand. "If mere looks could set me on fire, I'd be blazing away right now."

"You're immune to looks from me."

"Au contraire," he said in a lower voice, leaning forward. "You give me looks that can melt me or fry me to a crisp."

"I don't believe that," she said, but there wasn't any firmness in her voice, and warmth stole along her veins at his statement. Could she really have that effect on him? She turned away to look out the window in silence.

When they flew over Houston, the sun had set and lights had blinked on, a dazzling display far below. Ashley watched for a few minutes, entranced by the sparkle before she turned around. Her heart missed a beat when she met Ryan's steady gaze.

"I wondered if you're as dazzled as I am by this scene out the window, but I see you're not. You're burned out on flying, I suppose."

"No," he said, leaning closer. "I'll never get enough of this view," he said, looking directly at her.

She inhaled swiftly. "Stop flirting, Ryan."

"Why? That's the sizzle in life—getting to flirt with you, seeing where I can go with it, letting my imagination run."

She smiled and received an enticing, warm grin from him as he leaned forward to touch the corner of her mouth with the tip of his finger. "That's more like it."

The announcement from the pilot about landing broke into their conversation, and they both tightened their seat belts.

A uniformed driver in a limousine met Ryan and Ashley and drove them to a hotel. At the top-floor restaurant they were seated at a linen-covered table in a quiet corner. A pianist played old favorites in the background; candles burned at the tables; and fresh roses filled the centerpiece vases.

"If you're trying to impress me, you're succeeding," she said, watching two couples circling the small dance floor across the room.

"Good. I hope I can impress you a great deal more than this." Candlelight flickered, highlighting his prominent cheekbones and causing his black lashes to cast shadows there. If only he hadn't insisted on marriage, she thought, and then realized she was succumbing to the seductive trappings and to Ryan.

Their waiter brought menus, and after they had placed orders and were alone, Ryan stood and took her hand. "Let's dance before dinner," he suggested. Her immediate reaction was eagerness, swiftly tempered by caution as she placed her hand in his and went to the dance floor.

She walked into his arms and into memories of his lean, muscular body.

This was the second time she'd danced with him and it opened a Pandora's box of devilish longing that taunted her. Yet she was as conscious of the present as the past. She was aware of the warmth of his body, the cottony smell of his freshly laundered shirt, the strong column of his neck where her hand rested. Their legs brushed and she looked up to meet his gaze, and then couldn't look away, caught completely, enveloped in desire.

"Stop fighting me, Ashley," he whispered. "We're good together, and you know it. And this is the best of all possible solutions."

"Solutions? There, that says it all," she exclaimed. "Am I the problem? Is the baby a problem?"

"I'm going to try my damnedest to win you over, because I know it'll be worth every minute and all my efforts."

He pulled her closer, wrapping her in his arms and putting his head against hers. Dancing was marvelous, another irresistible temptation with him. She relished being in his embrace and swaying with him, and there was no way she could deny it. Recollections swirled like smoke as she recalled too clearly being held close in his embrace when they had been naked in bed. Steadily and slowly, bit by bit, he was taking chunks of her heart now.

When the song stopped, a faster number started and Ashley danced with him, sexual tension building as she watched him move around her. The devouring looks he gave her made her fluttery and conjured up more memories of seductive moments with him. She felt needed and knew he had turned on the charm to get what he wished, but underneath all that appeal was a man of steel who was going to get his way no matter what he had to do.

With a pounding heart, she gazed up at him and wanted him. In spite of all her anger, she thrilled to his kisses and enjoyed being with him.

When the dance ended, she turned abruptly for their table. He caught up with her and took her arm.

"Now maybe I've worked up some kind of appetite," he said when they'd sat. In minutes, he had his red wine and her water poured. He raised his glass in a toast. "Here's to a fabulous marriage," he said, waiting while she glared at him.

"How can you toast a sham marriage when you've coerced me into accepting?"

"Make the best of it," he said lightly, still waiting.

Exasperated, she picked up her glass, touched his and took a sip.

With deliberation he set down his glass and reached across the table. "Give me your hand."

Mystified, she did as he asked, watching his warm fingers encircle hers. "Since when do you want to hold hands through dinner? But then, I don't really know you."

"You will. We'll discover each other, and that's an exciting prospect. It'll be a fulfillment of dreams." His strong, warm hand closed gently around hers while he gazed into her eyes. "Ashley, marry me."

"You're asking again? I told you this morning I would. I assume *this* request comes with the same conditions."

He gave an almost imperceptible nod as he reached in a pocket and produced a box. Opening it, he slid a ring on her finger.

Five

How many times was he going to surprise her? Stunned again, she stared for a moment at the sparkling, enormous diamond on a wide gold band, surrounded by a spray of smaller diamonds.

"Great heavens!" she exclaimed. She pulled her hand away to look down at the ring, which dazzled her. "That's magnificent!" she exclaimed, glancing up at him. "I don't understand."

"What can't you understand?" he asked, momentarily frowning. "I want you to be my wife. I've given you an engagement ring to seal the promise."

"It's worth a fortune, and there's not one shred of love between us."

"Stop reminding me," he said somberly, and grasped her hand once more. "Look, I'll ask you again to give us a chance to let love flourish. I wouldn't do this otherwise."

She wished she could believe him, but she couldn't. "Ryan, if I weren't pregnant, you'd pull out of this engagement so fast I'd be in a spin."

Something flickered in the depths of his eyes, a confirmation to her of what she'd just declared. "I don't know what I'd do, because I like the idea of marriage to you," he said. "But that's beside the point. There's a baby to consider. Now, let's make some plans."

Shaking her head, she looked down at the ring, which was beautiful beyond her wildest dreams, and yet what she longed for, what was a lot more important than diamonds or a ring was his love.

Their waiter came and placed crystal plates with tossed greens in front of them.

As soon as they were alone again, Ryan took her hand once more. "Even if we break it off later, this will give the baby my name and a heritage. It will give me more rights to my child," he said quietly, and she heard a note of steel in his voice that chilled her.

"Are you going to try to take this baby from me?" she asked, wondering about his intentions. Now that she'd discovered he had a ruthless streak, she found him an enigma.

"Never. I couldn't ever hurt a child by taking it from its mother. This is my baby, and I'll love it. You should know that much about me by now."

"I know very little about you!" she exclaimed, and realized she needed to keep her voice down. Yet in spite of the remark she had flung at him, his statement relieved her beyond measure. "We didn't spend that weekend in chitchat."

"You know plenty about me," he reminded her, his tone changing immediately. His voice dropped and his words were slower, and she knew he was recalling their weekend together. "You've learned what excites me. You know how I look naked. You know—"

"Don't remind me!" she interrupted, wanting to stop words that conveyed their own magic and shifted the way she viewed him. "I don't have any idea what you truly care about. I don't like what you do when you're out of the bedroom. I don't know about your life or your family. That's more important."

"The prospect of learning about each other, and living together, I find fabulous. We've already started this and we'll build our relationship. That's a lifetime project."

"Ryan, does everything in your life go the way you want it to?" she asked. He reeked of success, and she wondered if failure was ever a concern for him.

"Of course not. Life doesn't unfold that way for anyone. But I get a reasonable return on my expectations. Now, let's set a date and make it soon. Before the wedding, you'll want to meet my father and brothers, and I need to meet your family."

She stared at him while her anger returned. She wanted to refuse and tell him to stop meddling. Instead, she looked down at the ring on her finger, which seemed like a shackle that bound her, heart and soul, to Ryan.

"I leave town tomorrow, but I'll be back late Friday night. That will give us the weekend to meet each other's family. When would you prefer to go see yours? Or would you rather have them come to Dallas?"

"We'll go there. I want you to see the farm. I'll call them first, of course. Saturday with my family would be a good time. It's a long drive, and I know them, they'll want us to stay the night," she said, realizing Ryan was going to charge right into marriage.

"We can stay, or I can drive back. I don't mind night driving. Do what you want."

"I can't believe you're even letting me decide," she said.

"I can yield on things."

Ashley shook her head. "Not on anything that really matters. But I'll probably want to return to Dallas. Let's try to arrive in late afternoon, because they eat supper and go to bed early."

As she talked, she watched couples circling on the dance floor, and others quietly eating. She felt caught in a dream that she couldn't wake from, yet it wasn't a dream. She glanced at Ryan, and when her attention shifted to his mouth, she realized she wanted to kiss him and feel his lips and tongue on her. She looked up again to see his knowing gaze.

"So what do you prefer to do?" he asked with a thicker voice, and she suspected that he had making love on his mind, too.

She tried to get back to his question and make a decision before Ryan did. "Let's go see your family on Sunday."

"Excellent," he replied, as he finished his salad and set his fork on his plate.

She had little appetite. His dark eyebrows arched in question. "You don't like your salad?"

"I'm not too hungry," she replied.

"Want to eat somewhere else?"

"Heavens no! This is a wonderful place. I just don't feel like eating."

"Okay," he said, withdrawing a slim cell phone. "Let's call and make arrangements. You can use my phone," he said, flipping it open.

Shaking her head, she got out her own phone. "I'll use mine. When I tell them I'm bringing a friend home, they'll know it must be someone special. But I'm not announcing this marriage over the telephone."

He smiled. "Whatever you want to do."

She glared at him, but then heard her father's voice and spoke softly, making arrangements to visit. Returning her phone to her purse, she waited while Ryan made his calls, watching his hand holding the tiny phone and remembering his hands on her.

"Grandma wants us there for supper Saturday night. I told her we'd try to get to the farm by five o'clock."

"Fine with me," he replied. "I'm looking forward to meeting them. My family will be at Dad's place Sunday evening about seven. We're set and this is good. At our wedding, I want my dad to be best man, and my brothers and Jake and Nick to be groomsmen. Is that too many for you?"

She shook her head. "No. I have Katie, Jenna and my cousin, and also a lifelong friend who still lives in my hometown."

"Now, let's pick a date. We might as well have this wedding soon," Ryan added.

She rubbed her forehead. "Will you slow down?"

"Why wait? You're pregnant, and the sooner we're wed, the better. What is there to wait for?"

"There are a million things," she snapped, clutching the tablecloth until her knuckles were white. "Like getting to know each other, for one."

He shrugged and waved his hand, dismissing her remark. "That'll happen. It's already starting. What weddings do you have scheduled next weekend?"

Her head reeled and she sat back, closing her eyes. "Next weekend!" she whispered. Why hadn't she guessed that Ryan would charge ahead full steam, like a barreling freight train?

"Ryan, I'm not getting married next weekend!"

"How about the weekend after that?"

"I have a night wedding."

"Can't your assistant manage, since you'll have advance notice? We'll be through with ours in time for her to go to the night wedding."

Ashley put her head in her hands and thought about her schedule and her meetings and the weddings, and what she would have to do. "September won't work?" she asked.

"There's no good reason to wait until September. How *about* the weekend after this?"

"Of course, why not?" she exclaimed. "You're getting everything else you want!"

He smiled and stood, taking her hand. "Let's go dance and cool down. Our dinners should be here when we return."

She went with him, again shocked by the speed with which Ryan was changing her life. "You're right on one thing," she said as they danced. "It's better to get out here and move around."

"Far better to hold you in my arms," he said softly, leaning down so his breath brushed her ear. "You look gorgeous tonight, Ashley."

"Thank you," she said, admiring the way the huge diamond on her finger caught and reflected the light. She turned her hand so she could stare at the ring, amazed he would give her such an expensive gift. "When did you get my ring?"

"This morning."

"You're rushing things, Ryan. I don't want to have sex right away. At least we can get to know each other before we do that." She leaned back to look up at him, and wondered what he was thinking.

"If that's the way you want it, that's okay. I can wait," he said. "I won't want to, but I can."

"Good. That's what I want very much. You've rushed me about marriage and the wedding, but sex is something that can come when we both want it. I've regretted my impetuous weekend with you."

"I'm disappointed to hear that, because I haven't had one shred of regret," he stated firmly. "Far from it. I thought it was the greatest weekend possible. That's why I couldn't forget you," he added.

His compliments flattered and warmed her, but she didn't care to encourage him.

"I have a request. I'll wait to have sex, but can we make an exception for our wedding night? This is my first, and hopefully only, wedding. It's a one-time event that I'll remember the rest of my life, and so will you. We can't ever go back and really do it again. So can we have a real wedding night?"

Her heart thudded and then raced. Two weeks until their wedding. Two weeks until they made love again. But if she succumbed and agreed to that, would she be able to resist him on other nights, before she got to know him better? Until they began to fall in love, or saw whether this sham marriage would explode in their faces and end as abruptly as it started?

She knew he was waiting. She thought again about what he'd said: "…first, and hopefully only, wedding…" Would it really be the only one? Did she want to have another night of sex with him, this time when he'd pushed her into marriage? She wanted patience and courtship and love. Instead, she had arrogance and a take-charge male who was determined to get his way. Was that who she wanted? Yet in fairness, she knew that tonight she *was* having courtship and romance from him. He was doing wonderful things for her family.

They danced around the floor in silence. Finally, she looked up at him. "All right, Ryan. We'll have a real wedding night."

"Fantastic!" he exclaimed. His eyes glittered with eagerness and he gave her a dazzling smile with a flash of white teeth, creases bracketing his sensual mouth. "Aah, I'll try to make you thrilled about that decision. I know *I'll* be happy." He pulled her close.

An actual wedding night. She thought about the tempestuous weekend she'd had with Ryan with all inhibitions gone, and her cheeks burned.

"Ashley..." He leaned back, starting to say something, and then his eyes narrowed as he looked at her. "You're remembering our weekend together, aren't you?" he asked in a husky voice.

She inhaled deeply and looked away. He tilted her chin up and gazed at her intently, with pinpoints of flame in the depths of his eyes. "I remember, too, and I want to love you by the hour. Ashley, this marriage can be damn good."

She closed her eyes, hurting inside. She wanted to shout at him that she needed love, not lust!

She pulled away from him and left the dance floor, hurrying to the table. He caught up with her immediately.

"Still angry with me?" he asked.

"Of course I am! Ryan, what we've got is lust and nothing much else."

"If I really thought that, I wouldn't go through with this marriage. But there are moments when your feelings for me do a complete turnaround. I think we can fall in love if you'll give us half a chance."

They ate in silence for a few minutes, and then he put down his fork. "Ashley, I'll pay for the wedding. I want to. I have enough money that you can hire who you need to get this pulled together in two weeks. Besides, since that's your area of expertise, it should be easy for you."

Her appetite was gone, anyway, so she placed her fork in her plate. "I assume we'll have a big wedding."

He nodded. "Afraid so. I have a lot of people I think I should invite."

"Our church at home isn't large. It probably holds about five hundred."

He rubbed the back of his neck. "I'll make a list, but I'm guessing about a thousand guests. Do you mind having the wedding at my church here in the city? We can go Sunday and you can look it over."

"It's all right with me. My family will understand. So will our friends, and a lot of them will think it's fun to come to Dallas for a wedding."

"I'll put your family, other relatives and attendants in my hotel, whoever is in the wedding party or close to you. Whoever you want."

"That's generous, Ryan."

He smiled. "I'm happy I can do something you like."

The man was a charmer, and she couldn't resist him. Already her anger wasn't as intense as it had been this morning. At least at moments it wasn't.

"The thought of doing it in two weeks makes my head spin."

"You're a professional wedding planner. You'll have all the money you want at your disposal. It shouldn't be too difficult for you," he remarked dryly.

"How do you know you can trust me not to bankrupt you?"

He smiled. "I suspect you're way too practical, far too honest and fair and unaccustomed to living lavishly."

"You're right," she said in surprise, and he grinned.

"See, Ashley, I'm getting to know you. If you'd set aside your anger, you'd get to know me."

"Oh, I'm getting to know you. Arrogant, self-assured—"

"I remember your description," he said, interrupting her as he stood and shed his coat, draping it over the back of his chair. "Since we're not going to eat, let's dance again."

He took her hand and led her to the dance floor for two fast numbers. She danced around him, watching his sensual moves, remembering his lovemaking, knowing exactly what he looked like beneath the brown slacks and snowy shirt.

At one point he reached out and pulled the clip from her hair so her blond locks tumbled across her shoulders. Dropping it into his pocket, he continued to dance, never taking his gaze from her.

How could she keep resisting him? she wondered. Even on the dance floor he was seductive, moving his hips in a sensual manner, while longing burned blatantly in his eyes. A band had appeared, replacing the piano player. The trumpet was loud and the drums had a throbbing beat that made her want to be as tempting to Ryan as he was to her.

Then it was a Latin number, and his sexy dancing intensified as she circled him. Sweat dotted his brow and his gaze undressed and caressed her, while she forgot her anger and the wedding and their future. There was only music and Ryan. Locks of his black hair fell over his forehead and he unfastened the top buttons of his shirt, loosening his dark brown tie slightly. Every move he made was evocative and she was on fire.

With a crash of drums, the song ended, and Ryan caught her, hauling her against him and leaning over her while he looked into her eyes. "I'm going to love you until you are drowning in need," he whispered, making her blaze with desire.

The band began a slow ballad. He swung her up and she moved into his embrace. Breathing fast, their thighs brushing, they held each other tightly. Fast and slow, the music played, and they continued to dance for another hour. Ashley was barely aware of anything around them—the other diners, the waiters, their table being cleared. Even the wedding had been temporarily forgotten.

Finally, when a number ended, Ryan took her hand. "If you want to get back to Dallas, we'll have to go now. Of course, if you want to stay the night, this is my hotel and we can have a suite."

She shook her head. "Let's get back to Dallas."

They returned to the table so she could get her purse, then left the hotel and rode back in the limo to the plane. As the jet lifted over Houston and she saw the splash of twinkling lights, her gaze shifted to the diamond on her finger. In one unforgettable day her life had changed forever, taking a turn she'd never dreamed would happen.

She was still stunned by all that had occurred, unable to lose her apprehension over Ryan's arbitrary ways. His profile, his straight nose and firm jaw indicated his determination to get what he wanted in life.

He was gazing out a window. He'd shed his coat and pulled off his tie, and had his shirt partially unbuttoned. She could see tufts of dark hair on his chest, and inhaled, remembering vividly how it felt to kiss and caress that chest.

With his long legs stretched out and his thick hair tangled by the wind, he was blatantly attractive.

She was marrying this man in two weeks! Whenever she thought about it, the realization stunned her. When he wanted something, he went after it exhaustively, and she'd better remember that. In this case, she knew it wasn't a wife he wanted, but his baby. She was merely a means to an end. But she had believed him when he told her he wouldn't ever try to take away her baby. Was she being foolish and gullible to accept that as truth and take him at his word?

One more reminder that she was marrying a stranger. Yet she was getting to know him. Most of the time their evening together had been exciting, and she'd had a great time.

She had to plan a large wedding for herself in two weeks. And then she would have a real wedding night with Ryan. Every nerve in her body tingled each time she thought about it.

As if he could sense what was on her mind, he shifted to face her and leaned forward, placing his elbows on his knees. "What are you thinking?"

"The wedding," she said, hoping he couldn't guess that she had been thinking about their wedding night.

"Shall we get back to some planning?" He glanced at the monitor and saw he could take off his seat belt. Standing up, he disappeared toward the front of the plane, to return a minute later with a legal pad and a pen. He handed them to her.

"You can make notes if you want. Monday, I'll give you a list of guests. I suspect you know everyone in that town you're from."

She nodded. "We just about do, but I don't intend to invite all of them."

"Do what you want. Get the dress you want. You can take care of all the details. I'll handle the honeymoon."

"Honeymoon?" she asked, startled. "Why? We're not in love, and I've asked for no sex after our wedding night. I can see the wheels turning in your mind. You expect to seduce me!" she declared.

"We'll get off by ourselves and get to know each other,"

he replied, leaning back in his chair. He looked as if he owned the world and expected everyone to do what he wanted them to. "Plan on a week."

"A week!" she sputtered. "Well, I'm not even going to argue with you about it," she said in exasperation. "Pick someplace warm and sunny. I don't like snow."

His enticing smile coaxed her to relax and stop fighting him. "See, we're getting to know each other."

"You don't have to continually remind me," she said. "What time of day shall we have the wedding?"

"Morning, and later we'll feed everyone lunch and have a blast. Then we're off on our honeymoon. How's that?"

"Fine with me," she said. "Rehearsal Friday night."

'You'll need help getting out invitations, won't you?"

She shook her head. "I can do it through my office and send you the bill."

He nodded, and she wondered if he was going to object to any plans she made, and suspected he wouldn't, no matter how exorbitant the price tag.

"Just remember, I have the baby's best interests at heart."

'You mean, you have Ryan Warner's best interests in mind," she snapped, and he leaned forward to put his hands on the arms of her seat.

"I have your concerns in mind, too. I promise you'll see that I do." His face was close, and her anger warred with her craving. Being with him was an emotional battle, while physically, there was only one response—desire. She looked at his mouth and thought about his kisses, and in spite of her anger at him, wanted to lean those last few inches closer and kiss him.

He moved nearer and his lips brushed hers. She shut her eyes and relaxed. When he covered her mouth with his, she moaned.

Snapping open the buckle of her seat belt, he pulled her to him, sitting back in his seat and lifting her to his lap, to hold her close while he kissed her hard. Ashley's heart pounded and her breathing became erratic. Forgetting their disputes, she wound her arms around his neck and kissed him in return, wanting so much more.

As they kissed, she knew time was passing and desire was growing more intense by the second. To slow things down, she pulled away reluctantly.

"You're irresistible, Ashley," he said gruffly, touching her throat.

"You know how I react to you," she replied, moving off his lap and straightening her clothes, sitting down to smooth her skirt and buckle up again. His steady look made her heart thud. Struggling for composure, she stared out the window at the black night, the pinpricks of lights occasionally showing in the distance.

"I don't know how you'll react," he replied solemnly after a few minutes' silence. He reached over to caress her cheek. "But I intend to learn how you respond to each touch and kiss."

"You're coming on strong, Ryan," she whispered, finding his words as effective as a touch. "Let's get back to some other topic. The wedding, if you want."

With a long, intense look, he shrugged. "We didn't discuss where we'll live after we marry. How about my condo? Then we can build a house, so we'll have more room when the baby comes, or soon afterward."

Astounded, she stared at him. "I hadn't thought about where we'd live," she said, thinking about his sprawling, plush condo in an exclusive, gated area. She also thought about her own place, which was smaller, far more simple. "That's fine, Ryan. None of this seems real to me."

"It's real," he said. "Come back over here in my lap and I'll convince you it's real."

She shook her head. "My mind boggles over all the abrupt changes. Things I never expected to have happen are occurring one right after the other."

"Also, in the next week, find a decorator. Do my bedroom over—colors, new furniture—so the place is both of ours. We should start married life with a new bed. Spend whatever you want."

She stared at him in consternation and amazement. "You can be so strong willed and then so generous."

"Maybe you'll discover that I'm really a nice guy."

"I know you're a nice guy," she said. "Until you want something."

He smiled. "You can do any other rooms over in my condo, too—or all of them if you want to."

She laughed. "You plunge full steam into everything you do! Okay, I'll look at your bedroom. A new bed for us would be great," she said, and the thought made her breathless.

"And I can't wait to try it out with you."

"You'll make me blush."

"Just makes you look even more gorgeous."

He fished in his billfold and handed her a card. "Charge everything you want to this."

"Ryan, you're being generous."

"You'll be my wife, Ashley. It's like doing it for myself," he answered casually. "Another thing we haven't discussed is your job."

"See?" she said. "This is what I was talking about. I knew you would step in and take charge of everything."

"I believe we're agreeing on most all of this. You know we have to make each one of these decisions. And I'm leaving a lot of the wedding plans solely up to you."

SARA ORWIG   89

In fairness, she knew he was right. "So what have you decided about my job?"

He gave her a fierce look that made her draw another sharp breath. "If you want to quit immediately, that's fine with me."

"No, I don't want to stop working yet."

"You have to before you have the baby. How about three months before, at the latest?"

"How about two?"

He nodded. "If that's what you'd like. As long as you're in good health, that's fine with me. And don't do any heavy lifting. I can send a man to help with any moving or carrying, since it's just you and two other females."

"I don't think we need a man," she said, smiling.

"Who carries those tall candlesticks and things like that for weddings? Who loads them into a truck and then into the church?"

She shrugged. "All right, I do or my assistant does. But I can't afford to pay some guy to hang around and carry stuff."

"I'll pay him. Give him some odd jobs around the place. I'll get someone who's young and strong and going to college, so he'll be part-time for you. How's that?"

"Fine, Ryan," she said, knowing it was useless to argue, and that it would be a big help to her. "Actually, I've thought about trying to get someone part-time for that very reason. It'll be good. I just didn't see how I could justify his pay."

"Now you don't have to."

"Thanks, Ryan," she said quietly. "You're being incredibly generous."

He shrugged. "I can afford to be, and we're going to be family soon."

She drew a deep breath and wondered how long it

would take her to adjust to her new status. They rode in silence for a time, until he asked her about growing up on the farm.

"What happened to your mother?" Ryan asked.

"She died in a fire in the barn when I was sixteen. She did a lot of farming, just like Dad. She loved it and so does my brother. What happened to your mother?"

Ryan smoothed his trouser leg over one knee. "We couldn't afford health insurance and she kept saying nothing was wrong. She had a stroke and died."

"How old were you?"

"Eighteen. Damn, I hated it."

"When that happened, you had your close friends, Nick and Jake, didn't you?"

"Yeah, and their friendship saved me. Emotionally and financially. We swore we'd help each other—I think I told you all about that."

"You did and it was amazing. All of you have success."

"Yeah, it's gratifying. Life has been generous to all of us. I don't ever want to be poor or hungry again. When I was growing up, we had some bad moments. But we were a tight family and all got along, and that's more than a lot of families have."

"Yes, it is. So did we, and I'm thankful for my family. Jeff, my brother, is twenty-one, four years younger than I am," she said. Ashley recalled that the weekend she'd met Ryan, she'd learned he was thirty-two.

They talked as they flew back to Dallas, and when they finally returned to her apartment, she faced him at the door. "It was quite a day and night, Ryan," she said solemnly, looking at her hand. "The ring is beautiful."

He brushed long strands of her hair from her face. "This marriage will work, Ashley. You'll see."

"You are the most supremely confident person I've ever known."

He shrugged. "I have strong feelings about our marriage."

"Our marriage, our baby… I can't get accustomed to everything that's happened. Thank you for dinner. The ring is spectacular, Ryan, but this is just crazy. You've given me this gorgeous ring, taken me dancing in Houston, and we're standing here politely saying good-night."

"You have other options," he said.

She shook her head. "I'm not ready for them." She slipped her arm around his neck, stood on tiptoe and brushed his cheek with a light kiss.

Instantly, he wrapped both arms around her and covered her mouth with his. His tongue stroked hers and she clung to him, all arguments and differences dissolving. In their place was a white-hot yearning—for more of his kisses, all of his passion, those hands and lips that could give her ecstasy. For a few minutes she gave free rein to her feelings, yielding to her hunger for him. When she finally pushed against his chest, he released her.

"That's all tonight, Ryan," she whispered. "Thank you, and I'll see you Saturday when you get back in town."

He nodded and took her key from her fingers to open her door for her. She stepped inside, switched off her alarm and faced him.

"Good night, Ashley," he said. In long strides he headed to his car. She watched until the motor started, and then she closed and locked the door. Leaning against it, she held up her hand, looking at the huge ring. Sadness, anger, amazement all filled her. With a ring on her finger and a wedding to orchestrate, she should be ecstatically happy, but she wasn't. She couldn't brush aside the concern she felt about Ryan for his high-handed ways.

Ashley wasn't tired yet, so she sat at her desk, writing memos, making notes, jotting numbers to call to make arrangements about flowers, food and music for the wedding. When she crawled into bed later, she lay in the dark, thinking about her future.

At least she could tell her family about the baby. She guessed all of them would be overjoyed.

Six

Saturday morning, sunshine streamed into Ashley's bedroom and she rolled over. She had one serene moment and then remembered all she had to do. She tossed aside the covers and got up to shower.

Shopping for a dress took only two hours. As she stood in front of the mirror, looking at the strapless white silk gown with a long straight skirt and removable train, she knew it was the one she wanted. While she stared at her reflection, she ran her hand over her tummy, which was still amazingly flat. She credited that fact to her height of five feet nine.

All during the morning as she shopped, made calls and planned, a gamut of emotions plagued her. One minute she would be apprehensive about a loveless union, and the next excited over the prospect of marrying Ryan.

At noon, while she dressed to go to the farm, another huge bouquet of mixed flowers arrived. She stared at the card and shook her head. The blossoms were beautiful, but they really held no meaning and couldn't calm her jitters about her future with Ryan. Far more meaningful had been his phone calls while he was in Chicago. They had talked long hours into the night, and each minute spent that way was a plus.

At two o'clock, when she swung open her door and Ryan stepped inside, her pulse gave its usual lurch. Dressed in a black knit shirt and black slacks, he radiated vitality. His gaze reflected his approval of her jeans and pink knit shirt. She wore her hair in one long braid. He placed his hands on her hips and studied her, turning her first one way and then another.

"Look at you in those tight jeans. Are you sure you're pregnant?"

"Very sure," she answered dryly.

He shook his head. "You don't look it in the least."

"I've decided it's because I'm tall," she said, while he continued to inspect her.

"You're beautiful, Ashley, and I'd rather stay here."

"Thank you. However, we're going to meet my family, who are waiting," she reminded him.

"I know, but you're too enticing in those jeans."

"Want me to find something baggy?"

"And spoil my day? Never! Let's go meet the family."

As they drove out of the city, Ryan glanced at her. "One topic we didn't settle. When do we announce that you're expecting a baby?"

"I've been thinking about it, and I'd just as soon tell the family now. I see no reason to announce it to others yet, but our families might as well know. And know why you're marrying me."

"Right there is a reason to wait to tell them."

She shook her head. "Now's the time, Ryan. When they find out why, your family will try to talk you out of this marriage, and that's okay."

"No, they won't. They'll know I'm doing what I want, and they know me well enough to realize that I wouldn't marry you simply because of the pregnancy."

She gave him an annoyed look of disbelief.

"You'll see, Ashley. I still say we'll have a good marriage."

"Without love, I don't see how."

"Every time you declare this union hopeless, I have to insist that I think love will come."

She bit her lip and looked out the window, knowing the futility of their continual dispute over the future. If only he would give love a chance to come, and then ask her to marry him!—then it would be a joyous event.

"I made arrangements with the church, and it's reserved when we wanted it," Ryan said. "I booked the country club and the band for the reception."

"We're moving right along, because I've arranged for the musicians for the wedding. I have the florist and have told him what I want. My dress is selected, along with what I'd like for the bridesmaids, and I've started my guest list. I need yours as soon as possible."

"I'll get it to you Monday afternoon. I can have my secretary pull one together, and I'll add to it."

"I've ordered cakes. Being a wedding planner cut days off making the arrangements, because I know what I want without having to pour through pictures and listen to descriptions. I could get a caterer for the reception, but I imagine the club will handle the food."

"They will. I told them you'd call to make arrangements," he said.

"And you don't care what I choose?"

"Not at all, and expense is no problem."

"Then it should be simple to arrange," she said. "As soon as we get the attendants confirmed, and the invitations in the mail, we'll be ready."

"I've reserved a private room at the club for the rehearsal dinner the night before and you can call them about the menu for that, too."

"Fine. Someday we'll have to think about baby names, but not this soon."

"I'll make a list of names I like and you do the same."

"And my guess is there won't be one name on your list that's on mine."

He smiled, glancing at her. "You think we're that different?"

"Absolutely," she declared.

He reached over to take her hand and place it on his warm thigh. Instantly, she thrilled to the intimate contact. "I'm eager for the wedding," he said in a husky voice. "And even more excited over the wedding night and loving you again."

She licked her lower lip, drawing her palm slowly along his thigh until she heard him inhale.

"Just a little more of that, Ashley, and I'm pulling off the road," he said hoarsely.

She withdrew her hand and returned it to her lap, gazing at the changing countryside as they sped east. Before long, the highway was lined with tall pines and thick woods.

When they approached the two-story, white farmhouse, she told him about its history. "Each family has built onto the place, but the original structure dates back to the late 1800s. The flood last year took some of the outbuildings and crops, but the house has never been in water."

"No regrets about leaving here?"

"Absolutely none. Farming is hard work. You're constantly fighting the elements. Maybe I still resent the farm for taking away my mother."

"Yeah, the way I blame hard times for robbing me of mine," he said gruffly. He took Ashley's hand. "Our baby is going to have opportunities, Ashley, and endless love."

For the first time she felt a bond with Ryan that had nothing to do with sex. A glimmer of hope flared as they shared feelings for the rough times in their pasts. She brushed a light kiss on his knuckles. "I hope you're right," she said. "I'll have to admit, we're alike about wanting to be in control."

Flashing a wicked grin, he chuckled. "So, you'll admit you like control just as much as I do."

"I suppose," she said, smiling at him.

When her father swung open the door, his blue eyes were filled with curiosity. "Ashley," he said, taking her into his arms for a hug. When he released her, she turned. "Dad, this is Ryan Warner. Ryan, please meet my dad, Ben Smith."

They shook hands and her father stepped back. "Come in. This is my mother, Ashley's grandmother, Laura Smith."

An attractive gray-haired woman in black slacks and a white cotton shirt stood behind him and smiled at them, causing crinkles around her large, blue eyes. Beside her was Ashley's brother, Jeff, who was also blue eyed and tall.

After introductions, they settled in the family room, with its high ceilings, braided rugs, family pictures and shelves of books.

Curiosity filled her father's eyes, but soon everyone was chatting, and her dad told tales about the farm and when Ashley and Jeff had been kids.

Looking relaxed and as if he had known her family for years instead of just an afternoon, Ryan relayed stories of his two-month stint on a horse ranch and his one attempt at bull riding, which had everyone chuckling. His stories were amusing, but Ashley realized that if he had done what he was telling them he had, he had a streak of a daredevil in him.

Over dinner, Ashley passed bowls of steaming mashed potatoes, thick brown gravy, slices of pot roast and hot biscuits. Ryan consumed a large enough amount of food to delight her grandmother, who liked serving guests and relatives.

As they relaxed after dessert, Ashley caught Ryan's attention and gave him a long look. "Folks, we have something to tell you," she said, pausing as all her family turned to her. "Ryan has asked me to marry him, and I've accepted."

Her grandmother gave a cry of joy and came around the table to give Ashley a hug, while her father and brother stood to shake Ryan's hand.

"Congrats, sis," Jeff said, grinning at her. "I didn't think this would ever happen."

She laughed, because she knew he was teasing her, and she was relieved to have made the announcement. When she turned to her father, she was surprised to see a solemn expression on his face, a searching look in his eyes.

Her first thought was that he knew she didn't want to marry Ryan, but he congratulated her, hugged her and gave her best wishes. They all adjourned to the family room, while she and Ryan answered questions and let everyone know the plans made so far.

Again she knew that if they were aware of all the circumstances, they would try to talk her out of it. Her father might not, because of the financial help Ryan would provide the baby.

She didn't want to wait until the end of their visit to tell them that news, but they wanted to hear wedding details and mark calendars. Finally, she thought there was a good moment, and she crossed the room to sit on the arm of her dad's chair. "We have another announcement that right now is for our families only," she said, gazing at Ryan, feeling as if she were in a dream. "We're going to have a baby."

Ashley's grandmother shrieked and hugged Ashley once more, while Ben shook hands with Ryan, congratulating him, before he turned to Ashley to hug her. He gazed at her again with a somber perusal. "That's the most wonderful news possible! I'll be a grandfather!"

His words contradicted his expression, but she was relieved anyway.

"Congrats, sis," Jeff said. "I'm going to be an uncle! That's sweet!"

They talked about the baby and the wedding, and then moved on to other topics.

Finally Ashley stood. "Anyone want a glass of water?" she asked. When no one did, she went to the kitchen. Jeff had discovered that Ryan played football, as he had. They both shared an interest in pro teams, and she left them talking avidly.

As she drank her water, she was surprised to see her father enter the kitchen and close the door.

Crossing the room to her, he placed his hands on her shoulders. "You're marrying Ryan because of the baby, aren't you?"

"I suppose I have to answer yes," she said quietly, not wanting to worry her dad, but finding it impossible to tell him anything except the truth.

"If there's no deep love between the two of you, think about what you're doing, Ashley. We're here for you. We'll help you with the baby, and you don't have to have Ryan Warner or his money in your life to get along."

"Oh, Dad!" she said, hearing the concern in his voice, and grateful for his support. She hugged him tightly, and he patted her back before she stepped away. "I hope we will learn to love each other," she said in a low voice.

"That's not much basis for marriage, Ashley. Think about it. It's good that he wants to marry you, but marriage is a relationship that takes a lot of strong bonding and co-operation on both parts. If you don't have that, you may be headed for disaster. Rethink this marriage. He's not the man for you. You're not glowing with happiness and love."

"I will think about it, Dad. And I have been. Ryan and I have discussed the situation at length," she replied cautiously, wondering how her father would react when he discovered Ryan was paying off the mortgage on the farm and would send Jeff to college. She patted her dad's arm. "Don't worry. I'll try to do what I think will be best for me and my baby."

He studied her intently before nodding. "I hope so, Ashley. I want to tell Ryan that I'd like to talk to him soon. Just the two of us."

"Oh, Dad, don't start a war with Ryan."

"I have no intention of doing any such thing. I just want him to know that he better not hurt you."

"He's not going to hurt me, and you're not going to intimidate him, either."

"I still want to talk to him. It won't hurt him to know how important you are to us."

She shook her head in exasperation, wondering why her life was filled with such strong-willed males. "Let's join the others," she said.

When she entered the family room again, she saw Ryan's questioning gaze. But he looked relaxed and had her brother and grandmother laughing at some story he was telling.

It was almost ten o'clock when they finally told everyone goodbye and got away, even though Ashley's dad kept urging them to stay the night and drive back the next morning.

"You have a great family," Ryan said in the car as they sped through the darkness. "The feeling may not be mutual, though. Your dad wants to see me, which is fine, but I don't think he's happy about our upcoming nuptials."

"No, he's not, but he'll change."

"He isn't prone to carrying a shotgun, is he?" Ryan asked lightly, and she smiled.

"No, he isn't. He's strong willed."

"Aah, now I know where you get it."

"That is really the pot calling the kettle black," she exclaimed.

"I'll be back to see your Dad Monday morning. He'll probably warn me not to hurt you, and I'll tell him that I'm paying off the mortgage on the farm."

"He may refuse you," she said.

"He won't. He's sensible, and it's been a hardship on you to help him. Your brother's sharp," Ryan continued. "I'd give him a job in a minute if he ever wants to leave the farm."

"Jeff is bright, and it's nice to know you'd hire him, but Dad's planning on Jeff taking over the farm. Jeff loves that farm more than anything on earth."

"I'm glad you don't," Ryan said, clasping her hand again.

They talked as they drove to Dallas, and as they approached her neighborhood, he glanced at her. "We could just go straight to my place," he murmured.

"No. It won't take you long to drop me off at home."

By the time they reached the door of her place, her desire for him was almost out of control, caused by his flirting, by spending the day and evening with him, by his touches and light kisses on her hand and cheek.

"Well, tomorrow morning I'll see your church. One thing at a time—"

He wrapped his arms around her and kissed her hard, his tongue plunging into her mouth. Ashley's heart thudded and she wrapped her arms around him, kissing him back. She moaned softly, wanting his lovemaking, aching for him in spite of all he'd done and his high-handed ways. She trembled in his arms and arched her hips against him, feeling his erection press against her, knowing he was ready for her.

Finally, she pushed against him and he released her. Both of them gasped for breath as she stepped away. "I'll see you in the morning," she said, and hurried inside, afraid that in another moment she might relent and invite him in.

She closed and locked the door, burning up with longing. She would be more than ready for the wedding night. What about all the honeymoon nights to follow? Was she going to toss aside her demands and give in to him?

Would love ever come for them? A deep, true love? Ashley suspected she was falling in love with Ryan, in spite of his arrogance and demands. Could he love her?

Wondering about her future, she switched off the light and went to bed.

Sunday evening, Ashley sat beside Ryan in his car again and looked at the residential area they drove through.

His father's condo was nestled in a gated area in a Dallas suburb. The place overlooked a large pond with fountains and elegant landscaping of willows and water birch.

"This is beautiful, Ryan."

"Dad seems to like it, which makes me happy," he said. "I'm happy to do things for your family, too, Ashley."

She studied him, wondering if she would ever figure

him out. He glanced at her and his eyebrows arched. "What? Why the puzzled scrutiny?"

"You can be so determined and cavalier, and then turn around and be so kind and generous."

"Makes life interesting, doesn't it?" he teased. There was a twinkle in his eyes, and she shook her head.

As they walked to the door, she hoped any nervousness she felt didn't show.

When the door swung open, she was surprised. Ryan's father was five inches shorter than his son. He was broad shouldered, barrel chested and had a deeply tanned face that was creased with wrinkles. His smile appeared genuine, and curiosity lit his thickly lashed green eyes as he took Ashley's hand and shook it.

"Ashley, meet my father, Zach Warner. Dad, this is Ashley Smith."

"Come in. I'm happy to meet you, Miss Smith."

"Please, just call me Ashley," she said, although she knew she couldn't address him as anything except Mr. Warner.

"For once your brothers are here ahead of you. I suppose you've got them curious to meet your friend," Zach said.

They walked through the entryway, with its polished hardwood floor, into a large family room with leather furniture and a wide-screen television. Two men stood and she knew she wouldn't have picked them out to be Ryan's relatives, either.

"Brett, this is Ashley Smith," Ryan said, as a tall, thin man with blond hair came forward to shake her hand. The shared family characteristic was their green eyes. Ryan turned to a brown-haired man, who was much shorter and stocky. "This is my baby brother, Cal."

"Welcome, Ashley. We're already impressed, because you're the first woman Ryan has brought home to meet us.

We've never figured out whether he's embarrassed about us or embarrassed about the women in his life."

"I'm going to be embarrassed about you if you don't stop," Ryan joked, and they all laughed.

"Please have a seat," Zach said, and then Brett offered drinks. Ashley requested her usual glass of water.

After they politely asked about her family and job for a while, Brett crossed the room to her. "Well, lookie here," he said, taking her hand, with the engagement ring. He glanced at her and then at Ryan, who shifted closer to her on the sofa and draped his arm around her shoulders.

"You're as observant as your brother," Ashley said, smiling at Brett.

"Dad, y'all, we're engaged. Ashley is going to marry me," Ryan announced, and from his tone and manner, she didn't think anyone would guess their true situation.

Ryan's dad let out a whoop and came to hug her. "Welcome to the family!" he exclaimed, with so much warmth, she hurt. Everything that happened made her yearn for true love. This sham marriage was a cheat, robbing Ryan, as well as her. Why couldn't he see that?

"That's the best news I've had in years," Zach declared.

The brothers congratulated Ryan, good-naturedly gave her condolences, and their mood became more festive.

Finally, everyone sat down again and they talked about the wedding, then moved on to other topics.

As she listened to the brothers chatting, Ashley felt more reassured about Ryan. He had a good relationship with his father and siblings, with a lot of light bantering going on. Yet they included her in the conversation. She enjoyed them all and knew she had one less worry, one less blank spot about her fiancé.

Finally, Ryan glanced at his watch, stood and reached for her hand.

"Before we leave, folks, we have one more announcement that, at this time, is for family only." Ryan looked down at her and his green eyes were warm, surprisingly filled with pride. His expression would convince anyone that he was happy over the announcement he was going to make.

"Dad, you're going to be a grandfather! You guys will be uncles."

Chaos ensued with the brothers whooping and congratulating them, and Ryan's father giving Ashley another hug. He had tears in his eyes as he gazed at her. "I can't tell you what this means, Ashley. I had given up on these guys and resigned myself to never having grandkids. I can't tell you how happy this makes me."

"I'm so glad," she said, smiling at him. "We're excited about it, too."

Cal and Brett slapped their brother on the back, thanking him for getting them off the hook with their father, while Ryan beamed with such convincing joy that she felt another pang, wishing they were truly in love, wondering what his family would think if they knew this marriage was taking place because Ryan had coerced and bribed her. As she watched him with his family, it was difficult to reconcile the friendly, relaxed son and brother with the determined, arrogant male who would go to such lengths to get his way.

It was another two hours before they got away, and as they drove off, all the men stood in the yard, waving at them.

"You have a great family, Ryan," she said with sincerity.

He grinned. "You sound surprised."

"No, I just didn't know."

"So now maybe I'm one small degree more acceptable."

She didn't answer, thinking about all that had happened

between them. He picked up her hand and brushed a warm kiss across her knuckles. "Stop worrying so much, Ashley."

"I'm trying, Ryan," she answered. "It's difficult," she said, thinking about his father and brothers.

"It's obvious that at some point in time, about four months back, you found me likable," he said dryly. She started to pull her hand free, but he tightened his grip.

"Calm down, Ashley. You're annoyed because you want to make every single decision yourself. Let me hold your hand." He raised it to his lips to brush another kiss there.

"By the end of two weeks, I'll be a wreck with wanting you," he said in a hoarse voice that set her nerves humming.

"The two weeks will fly by," she said, thankful for all she had already accomplished.

"Not quickly enough for me."

At her door he gave her a light kiss and left. As she moved around, getting ready for bed, she thought about all that had happened during the weekend. Ryan had a great family, and she was more relieved over that discovery than she'd let him know. She realized that the more she was with Ryan and the more she learned about him, the more likely it was that she would fall in love with him. She paused with her nightgown in hand.

Was she already in love with him? They were together constantly now, and everything she learned seemed to increase his devastating appeal. They were opposites in so many ways, yet they were compatible, too, about families, schools for their baby, dancing and even being together, when marriage wasn't the issue. He had always made her heart pound just by being there. But were her feelings for him stronger now because she was more involved with him? Was she already in love with Ryan, when he didn't love her in return?

Seven

Two weeks later, on Saturday morning, Ashley stood in front of an oval mirror in the bride's dressing room at Ryan's church. She gazed at herself, while her grandmother stood beside her smoothing out her veil. "You look so beautiful, Ashley. If only your mother could see you!"

"You look pretty, too," she said, thinking her grandmother did look lovely in her slim-fitting rose silk dress, her silver hair turned under. On her shoulder was a gardenia corsage from Ryan. "I can't believe this day is actually here."

"It is, and it's time for me to go, since I'll sit in front, in your mother's place." She placed her hands on Ashley's shoulders. "I wish you all the happiness in the world. You must be marrying a fine man, Ashley. He's been amazingly generous and kind to us. I know about the mortgage and about his offer to send Jeff to college."

"Dad seems to be happy and grateful. I was afraid he would refuse to let Ryan help."

"I think Ryan convinced him that we're part of his family now and he's part of ours, so it's all the same. But of course, it never really is. You're fortunate, Ashley. You're marrying a fine man."

"I am, Grandmother," she answered, feeling thoroughly insincere, wanting to cry that she really didn't know Ryan that well, and they didn't love each other. Or at least, he didn't love her.

She turned to hug her grandmother, wondering what would have happened if she had told Ryan no. It was too late for such speculation now. She stepped back, and Laura straightened Ashley's train.

"This is a gorgeous dress and perfect for you. Now c'mon, girls, it's time," she said to the bridesmaids, who wore yellow sheath dresses and carried bouquets of mixed spring flowers with huge yellow tulips.

They filed out with her grandmother, and Ashley turned back to the mirror to look at herself, unable to believe what she saw in the mirror. She fingered the exquisite gold fili-greed necklace entwined with diamonds and pearls that Ryan had presented to her last night.

Ashley knew her father was waiting, and in minutes it would be time for her entrance. But she wanted a moment to compose herself.

There was a knock on the door, and she assumed someone had come to get her. She turned, expecting her father. "Come in," she called. The door swung open and Ryan's redheaded friend, Kayla Landon, entered.

Startled, Ashley felt a chill as she turned. "If you're looking for the sanctuary, it's down the hall to the right."

"No, I'm looking for you," Kayla said in a soft voice,

and again, Ashley was amazed that Ryan had wanted so badly to marry, because this woman was stunning. She wore a gorgeous, skintight white silk dress with embroidered red rosebuds along the neckline and the hem. Her hair was curled, hanging to her shoulders. She had flawless skin; rosy cheeks; a full, pouty mouth; thick eyelashes; and a figure that should turn all male heads at the wedding.

As Ashley looked at her, she suddenly no longer felt so pretty, and her dress seemed incredibly plain and simple in comparison.

"I wanted to congratulate you on catching Ryan," Kayla said, coming into the room and closing the door behind her. "That's quite a coup. You're not in his social class and you're definitely not his type. We all know that he's marrying you out of pity," she said with a smug expression.

Ashley had started to reach for her bouquet, preparing to leave, but she halted abruptly in shock.

Kayla came close enough for her perfume to reach Ashley. "I never dreamed a pregnancy would do it," Kayla continued. "You know he doesn't love you. That's the only reason a man like Ryan would marry you."

Ashley clamped her jaw more tightly as a knot closed her throat. The only way Kayla could know about the pregnancy was from Ryan. He had broken a trust, and at that moment she hated him for it.

"Of course, he'll marry you, but if you think he'll stay faithful, think again," Kayla purred, smiling slyly. "If he can't stay faithful before the marriage, he won't stay true after, and you might as well know now what you're getting into. I'm sure you don't care, though, as long as you get some of his money. He ought to insist on a paternity test, however, to make sure he's the father."

"Get out, Kayla!" Ashley snapped, hating the tears that

threatened. "Get out!" She looked around for something to throw at the woman whose eyes widened before she turned to yank open the door again, her laughter floating behind her.

"Of course, it's never too late to back out. And I'm definitely not out of his life." She closed the door.

Shaking in dismay, Ashley dabbed at her tears, knowing she was streaking the light makeup she wore. Ryan hadn't been faithful. He had shared the secret of her pregnancy with Kayla, when only their families were supposed to know. That hurt worse than anything.

Ashley clenched her fists. She couldn't go through with this sham wedding! It wasn't too late. She could run away right now, and explain to her family and friends later. It would prevent this wedding from happening, and save her from marrying a man she couldn't trust.

She reached behind her to unfasten Ryan's necklace and throw it against the wall. She hurt all over and didn't want to marry him, no matter what he did or what happened.

She was reaching back again to free the top button of her dress, when she paused. Could she hurt so many people—Ryan's family, her family, the baby? Or marry him and take his financial support and have an easier life—would that be better?

Someone rapped on the door. "Ashley, it's time," her brother called. "Everyone's waiting."

Numbly, she picked up her bouquet of white orchids and white roses. She walked slowly to the foyer, while her father came forward with a somber expression. He tilted her chin up.

"You don't look happy," he said gruffly, unable to hide his worry. He dug in his pocket and withdrew keys. "Honey, you can walk right out the door now. Take my car and go, and I'll explain for you. Don't enter into a marriage that'll make you miserable. You can back out this minute and I'll stand by you. Take my car keys."

With a heavy heart she stared at the keys in his open palm. She could walk away and her father would give her his support. Did she want to escape this marriage to Ryan? Because here was her last chance before taking a vow.

Had something gone wrong? Ryan knew time was passing.

While he stood at the altar, he reminded himself to be patient. Maybe it was something with Ashley's dress or hair that had delayed her.

The bridesmaids were in place and the organist was improvising, playing the same music repeatedly.

Right now, their wedding night seemed a thousand hours away instead of the end of the day. Ryan's father stood beside him, and Nick and Jake were lined up beyond his dad and brothers. Ryan glanced over the large crowd. His church was beautiful, with rock walls, a vaulted ceiling and a huge pipe organ. The carpet was a brilliant blue and sunshine poured through the stained glass windows, which glowed like multicolored jewels, but he barely noticed his surroundings. He wanted to glance at his watch. Ashley was late, which was uncharacteristic of her.

Where was she? Had something happened? Was she having cold feet at the last minute? Worries plagued him and he thought about the moment this morning when he had been seized by the feeling that he had pushed Ashley too hard into this wedding. But then he'd come to the same conclusion he always had, that marriage was the best for all concerned.

Should he have waited and courted her, and married her after the baby's arrival?

Too late now, unless she had run out on him. He shifted his weight slightly, wanting to leave and go find her. He'd heard of runaway brides.

And then he saw her appear in the narthex and take her father's arm. They stood talking, and Ryan wished they would begin. Finally, the organist received the signal that the bride was ready.

As Ashley walked toward him down the aisle, all of Ryan's worries and apprehensions vanished. His mouth went dry and his heart pounded. He remembered the first hour he'd met her at a party, and how he'd been drawn to her easy smile and open friendliness with everyone. The attraction between them had been instant and intense.

Today she looked stunning, incredibly beautiful, and he didn't have a qualm or doubt that he was doing the right thing. He couldn't imagine that they wouldn't fall deeply in love.

She was ravishing, sexy, independent. So far as he could discover, she had great qualities. He liked her family. Reassured they were doing the best possible thing, he watched her. He wanted her to himself, and knew this would be one of the longest days of his life until he could get her away for their honeymoon.

As she drew closer, he frowned. She was pale as snow and wouldn't look at him.

Surely this wasn't her anger stirred up all over again. Last night at their rehearsal dinner, she had seemed to have a great time, and had kissed him thoroughly before she'd told him good-night. Yet as her father placed her hand in his, Ryan knew something was dreadfully awry. Her father's expression reinforced his suspicions.

When they turned to repeat their vows, Ryan clasped Ashley's icy hands and glanced at her bare throat. Where was the diamond-and-pearl necklace he had given her the night before? She had seemed thrilled with it, and said she'd wear it today, but no necklace adorned her throat now.

Ryan couldn't wait to talk to her, and tried to concentrate on their wedding, knowing he should pay attention. Yet there was no way that Ashley was enjoying one minute of it. What had happened?

Finally the minister pronounced them man and wife. He introduced them to the crowd and they swept up the aisle. Ryan held Ashley's arm and motioned to an usher. "Tell the photographer that we'll be right back for pictures," he said, before turning to her. "Come here," he ordered, and tugged lightly on her arm. She went with him down a long hall, and the first empty room he could find, he stepped inside. Closing the door behind them, he gripped her shoulders and leaned down to look directly into her eyes.

"What's wrong?" he asked.

She gazed at him with a glacial expression. "I don't know why I thought I could count on you. This marriage isn't built on respect and trust."

"What are you talking about? Trust me about what?"

"To be faithful. To not announce that I'm pregnant and that you have to marry me."

Shocked, he frowned. "What on earth are you talking about? I haven't done any such thing. There hasn't been another woman in my life since you came into it. The only people I've told about your pregnancy were our families, when you were with me."

"Please!"

"That's the truth! Where's all this coming from?"

"Kayla came to see me before the wedding—"

"Dammit!" Fury boiled in him over a woman from his past that he couldn't shake out of his present. "You listened to her?" His anger intensified, hot and swift and blinding, but was followed instantly by common sense and relief. "Ashley, there's not one shred of truth in anything she said to you. I swear, there isn't. I wish I'd never met her."

Ashley's eyes widened as she searched his gaze.

"Kayla is over and out of my life, whether she likes it or not," he insisted. "There hasn't been anyone—"

"How'd she know that I'm pregnant?"

Surprised, he slid his hands down Ashley's upper arms. "Darlin', I don't know what she said to you, but I'd say that she was guessing. If you'd denied being pregnant, she would've shrugged it away. Knowing you, I doubt you contradicted her. I swear to you that I didn't tell her that you're pregnant, nor have I been unfaithful to you."

"She said I wasn't in your class, and the only reason you'd marry me was out of pity, since I'm pregnant."

"Dammit, forget all that rubbish about class. I've told you about my past. I came from nothing. I'm not of one class and you another. That's absurd. It sounds feudal. You have a great family. I like them and I'm not marrying you out of pity or sympathy or any such thing. Kayla guessed the pregnancy. Did you confirm it?"

"No. I was stunned," Ashley replied quietly. "Her accusation of your being unfaithful isn't true. Or am I being naive to ask?"

"Hardly. I told you, there hasn't been anyone for a long time, definitely not since you've been back in my life. Nothing Kayla said was the truth," he insisted. "I promise you."

Her gaze searched his and he waited quietly, knowing she was weighing what he'd said against what Kayla had told her. "I almost left this morning," Ashley admitted.

"Thank heavens you didn't!" he exclaimed. "Okay, now?"

While silence again stretched between them, he gazed

into her eyes, until she nodded. "Okay. I may be the most gullible woman on earth, but I'll accept what you're saying."

"Ashley, time will show you that I'm truthful. C'mon, let's go enjoy our wedding."

"All through the ceremony I kept thinking I was making a mistake. I barely heard what the minister said."

"I'm sorry Kayla ruined your wedding for you. She's out of my life. I hope you heard the minister pronounce us man and wife."

"I heard that," Ashley said solemnly.

Ryan looked at her features and her hair. "You look stunning today. I'll remember you forever the way you look now."

She smiled, and he smiled in return. "Let's give each other half a chance," he added. "I expect us to fall in love."

"I hope you're right."

"Did you hear him say, 'You may kiss the bride'?" Ryan asked, his desire spiraling as he looked at her full, soft mouth.

"Yes, I did," she answered, with that sultry quality in her voice that excited him even more. He leaned the last few inches to kiss her, and her mouth opened to him as she wrapped her arms around him. Her kiss aroused him, and he longed to be alone with her. He wanted her naked in his arms, in his bed.

A pounding on the door got through to him dimly above the roaring of his pulse, while Ashley pushed against his chest and wiggled away. "Ryan!" a deep voice called.

"That's Brett." Ryan reached around her to open the door, and his brother stepped inside.

"Sorry," he said apologetically to Ashley. "They're searching for both of you for pictures. You're holding up the works."

"Yeah, yeah, we're coming," Ryan answered, wishing

he could pick her up and run out the back with her, sweeping her away right now. He took her arm and they started to follow Brett, then stopped again.

"Everything okay now?"

"Yes," she said, smiling at him. Yet there was still a wary look in her eyes, and he wondered how much damage Kayla had done.

"Where's the necklace I gave you?" he asked.

Her expression was stricken and her hand flew to her throat.

"Ryan, it's—" She bit her lip and blinked. "I'm so sorry. I threw it on the floor of the room where I dressed. Let me go get it."

He shook his head. "I'll have Cal or Brett find it. Don't worry. The necklace isn't what's important here." He received a warm look at that, and felt better, hoping they'd cleared the air between them.

During the picture taking Ryan kept his arm around Ashley's waist as much as possible, wanting her close at his side. The minute they reached the club for the reception, he was separated from her by crowds of friends and relatives, who congratulated him and wished him well. Often, he could spot Ashley across the room, and occasionally, she would look around and make eye contact. He could feel the invisible electricity instantly generated, and fought a constant urge to glance at his watch.

Finally she was at his side and it was time for the first dance. He took her hand as they made their way to the dance floor. She had shed the train of her dress, and followed his lead easily.

"I want to take down your hair and peel you out of that gown and kiss you all night long," he said, knowing he ought to avoid the erotic images of her that he had thought about so much today. "You're in my whole being, like a heady wine, Ashley."

"Ryan, everyone is watching us now. I hope they can't hear you."

"You know they can't. You're beautiful, and I dream about having you in my arms. This is torture, and it'll go on how many more hours?"

She laughed. "Most of the afternoon. We just got started. According to you, this is a once-in-a-lifetime event, so relax and enjoy it."

"There are some other things I would rather be doing," he said tersely. "The first minute we can feasibly get out of here, let me know and we're off."

"So you said you'd surprise me about where we'll go for our honeymoon. When are you going to tell me?"

"Not until we're on our way."

"Which we won't be for hours," she said, and her tone had lightened, which cheered him.

Ryan drew Ashley close, wanting to wrap her in his embrace, but she pushed against his chest. "Everyone is watching, so show a little more propriety."

"Propriety isn't my strong suit," he said with amusement as they circled the dance floor.

She danced with him, wondering about their future. Would they fall in love? Would Ryan be able to settle into marriage and give up his playboy lifestyle and beautiful women? The last was a question that constantly nagged at Ashley. Marriage was an abrupt alteration for him, even more than the disruption to her own life. Kayla's accusations had unsettled her, and she couldn't dismiss them with the cavalier nonchalance that Ryan had. And was she being foolishly gullible by believing him instead of Kayla?

Ashley realized then that to feel that strongly about him with Kayla, she must be in love with Ryan. How had love for him engulfed her so swiftly? She had her answer in memories, as well as when she looked at him.

Searchingly, she met his gaze. She guessed he would be a wonderful father, but she couldn't imagine him being a devoted husband when there was no love, at least on his part, and he was accustomed to women and freedom.

She looked at her hand in his. Hers was pale, smaller, her fingers slender next to his. Her ring sparkled in the bright lights of the ballroom.

She remembered Jake and Emily's wedding. When Emily had confided that it was purely a marriage of convenience, Ashley had wondered how her friend could bear to go into such a union. Yet here she was, locked in one almost like that herself. All the reassurances she had poured out for Emily seemed hollow and empty now.

Yet as she danced, hope grew. Now that Ryan had insisted she should ignore Kayla, the future once again held possibilities.

He was watching her, and she tilted her head and smiled up at him.

"So you're happy now?" he asked.

"Ryan Warner, you made me marry you. Well, I'm going to make you fall in love with me. Hopelessly in love."

Excitement flashed in the depths of his gaze and his dark eyebrows arched. "That's a promise I look forward to. It makes my day even more than the wedding."

"You'll see," she said, smiling at him and meaning what she said.

In minutes the dance ended and he led her back to the sidelines, where her father claimed her and Ryan turned to ask Laura to dance.

"I'm worried about you, Ashley," Ben said when they were on the dance floor. "It's good to have Ryan's financial support, but that's not enough for marriage. Just remember, I'm always here for you, day or night."

"I know, Dad. I'm fine. There was something disturbing this morning, but it's all right now."

"Good. I'm glad to hear it. I wish you all the happiness in the world," he said, and she smiled up at him.

"Thanks. I love you," she said. Her gaze went past him to Ryan, who was charming her grandmother, she was sure. Tall, exuding self-assurance, radiating vitality, he seemed convinced that all would go well. His confidence was contagious, and she knew she was falling under his spell.

Next, Ryan's father danced with Ashley, while Ryan stood on the sidelines and watched. He wanted the event to end. He was eager to get Ashley to himself, and this reception was stretching his nerves.

The minute the dance was over Ryan took her arm. "They want us for a picture or some such," he said, leading her toward the nearest door.

"Ryan, the photographer is over by the cake."

"So he is. If you must know, that was just an excuse to get you alone. C'mon. Let's slip away for one quick kiss," he said, taking her into a room across the hall and turning her to him as he leaned down to kiss her. She clung to him, responding as always to his kisses, setting him on fire. Her mouth was soft and she wore an enticing scent. Her shoulders were bare, tantalizing soft curves showing at the straight neckline of her dress. Now she was his wife. With every moment that passed he grew more certain they had done the best thing possible, and to his surprise, he was growing pleased with the whole prospect.

"We have to get back. This is our party and we're host and hostess," she whispered, pushing against him.

Ryan inhaled deeply. "It seems like an eternity until we can get out of here," he told her again. "Just one more quick kiss." He pulled her to him, sliding his hand down her back to cup her bottom. His breathing was ragged and he ached.

Finally, he reluctantly released her, and this time, she stepped away from him. "Ryan, we're going back to the party," she said firmly. "You'll have to wait."

He looked at her features as if memorizing them, then nodded. She took his hand and led him inside the ballroom, and minutes later she was surrounded by old friends and Ryan was across the room.

He tried to pay attention to friends talking to him, but all he could do was think about Ashley and glance at her constantly. She was laughing at something someone said to her. When had any particular woman been this important to him? He knew the answer to his own question, never before, and that made him all the more certain he'd done the right thing in forcing her to marry him. Every time they kissed, she responded to him fully. They enjoyed each other's company and they liked each other's families, all of which meant they were truly bonding. But it was already deeper than that. He trusted her and knew he could confide in her. He could tell her his hopes and plans, and he valued her opinion when they discussed topics. Most of all, she set him on fire with her passion.

No sex after their wedding night… He was certain after making love tonight, she wouldn't hold out in the days to come. Sex would be fantastic and make the ties between them stronger. How could they keep from falling in love?

He turned and Kayla was there. His irritation surfaced, but it was mild because she was no longer important and nothing she said mattered. "I heard what you told Ashley," he stated.

She shrugged. "I figured you wouldn't marry her unless she's pregnant. And if she's not, well, I don't think you'll be able to stick with one woman either way. Particularly one who isn't in your social world, Ryan. You're not going to settle down and be the sweet, faithful husband," she said, smiling slyly at him.

"It's over between us, Kayla. Absolutely and forever."

Her smile widened and she licked her lips slowly. "Darling, you'll be back. I give you three months tops." Her strong perfume assailed him when she stood on tip-toe and brushed his cheek with a kiss. Stepping away, she smiled at him.

"You stay away from Ashley," he declared again, wondering how he could have ever been so involved with Kayla.

Still smiling, she turned and walked off.

One of his brothers called to him, and Ryan joined Brett and a group of friends who stood nearby. He forgot about Kayla, because Ashley filled his thoughts. His gaze drifted across the crowd until he spotted her. Talking and laughing, she stood in a group of guests. He wondered if he would ever tire of looking at her.

He glanced at his watch. "C'mon, Ashley."

Ashley glanced around and saw Ryan talking with his brother and some other men. Nick Colton stood in the group, and she saw Jake Thorne join them. She had gotten to know Jake because of planning his wedding, and now Jake had been a groomsman in her own. He had rugged features that softened when he smiled. He was friendly, but she felt he was reserved, keeping strangers at arm's length. All three men shared that same determination and poise, and she wondered if they had ever clashed in the years they had been friends.

She looked at her tall husband. She had seen Kayla talking to him only a short time before. When she'd seen the redhead brush his cheek with a kiss, Ashley hurt briefly. She had never been jealous in her life, but it pained her to watch Kayla kiss him even lightly.

Had Ryan really meant all he'd said? She would take him at his word until she had a reason not to, but again, she hoped she wasn't being foolishly gullible. Even though Ryan had been convincing and reassuring, uncertainty still hovered in the back of her mind.

She watched him while she half listened to those around her. He was charismatic and exciting, and she still couldn't believe that she was Mrs. Ryan Warner.

Ryan's wife. The whole world seemed different now. If only... She couldn't stop wishing that there was mutual love between them.

They would have a real wedding night. The thought turned her knees to jelly and heated her insides, because she could remember their weekend and what a consummate, energetic lover he had been. She pulled her thoughts back to the present and looked at Ryan, meeting his gaze. Even though he was across the room and people were between them, sparks flew. She smiled and saw him wink at her in return, and her eagerness to be alone with him mushroomed.

The hours dragged until finally she decided it was time to go. Last-second jitters sent a tingle up her spine.

She worked her way around the room, and when she reached Ryan, she took his hand.

He turned to look at her and excused himself from those around him. She led him to the dance floor and stepped into his arms.

"We can leave now, but I wanted one last dance," she said, and saw a flare of satisfaction in his expression.

"Aah, that's the best news since the minister pronounced us man and wife. And it's not as if we can't dance on our honeymoon."

"This is magical, Ryan. I want to dance and remember it," she said.

"I'm encouraged if you're really enjoying yourself and want memories of today." He wrapped his arms around her and held her tenderly while they danced to the slow number. "This is the beginning, Ashley. Life will be good between us."

"I hope so," she answered solemnly, her heart thumping over his words, and hope kindling that his love would blossom.

The minute the music ended, he took her hand. "C'mon, Ashley, we've partied and danced and schmoozed all afternoon. I finally can have you all to myself."

"Let's tell our families goodbye before we go, and let a few other people know."

He groaned. "That'll take another hour."

"But that's what we're going to do," she insisted.

"Let's just get away and let them all party. Look— everyone is having a grand time. They won't even know," Ryan urged.

"As if you can slip away from anything without being noticed! No, we'll say goodbye and give our friends a chance to throw balloons at us."

It *was* almost an hour later when Ryan took her hand and they dashed to the waiting limo, past their well-wishing guests. Their driver sped away toward the airport.

Ashley had given a dress to Ryan to have ready for her later and as soon as they were airborne, she changed to a pale blue silk sheath.

"You look as beautiful as ever," he said when she returned to sit by him. He had shed his coat and sat facing her with his long legs stretched out.

"Thank you," she replied. "Now you have to tell me where we're headed for our honeymoon."

He leaned forward to take her hands in his. His hands were warm and he looked surprised. "You can't be cold! Nervous?"

"Maybe a little," she conceded. "This is a giant commitment."

"New and wonderful," he said, surprised at himself because he not only hadn't expected to be married at this age, but he never would have guessed he could be so happy about it.

"Tonight we'll stay at one of my hotels in Houston, and tomorrow we'll fly to my villa on the Yucatan Peninsula."

"How many homes do you own?" she asked, constantly reminded of how little she knew him.

"I have my condo and this villa. Everywhere else, I stay in a hotel."

"I hope you're right about marrying like this, Ryan," she said solemnly, and he reached out to take her hand and pull her onto his lap. She glanced at his mouth, wanting his kisses, yet intending to wait until they were off the plane and alone.

"I know I"m right," he said, carefully beginning to take her hair down, removing first one pin and then another to let her long blond hair fall free.

She grasped his wrist. "I'll look all mussed up when we go into the hotel."

"You'll look absolutely gorgeous. I like your hair down, so it might as well be that way sooner rather than later," he said, while pulling out another pin. He tilted her face up to his. "Not still angry with me, are you?"

She shrugged. "Not about Kayla."

"Thank heavens. I'd forgotten about her. I hope you will. She's history, Ashley."

"Good. I still can't keep from wishing we'd waited for love to come first."

"It will," he said with his usual assurance. "And I look forward to when you tell me I was right."

"You may prove to be correct, but your method was too cavalier. You're too strong willed and certain you're right. If you'll stop making every decision for me, I'll be a lot more happy."

"I had no idea that I was doing so. You've seemed pretty damn independent."

"Not since I met you," she argued, releasing some of her pent-up feelings.

"We're not going to quarrel today," he said, his voice dropping as he twirled a strand of her hair in his fingers. "You looked fantastic for the wedding," he added in a deeper tone. "I'll never get tired of just looking at you."

"Yes, you will," she said, smiling at him, warmed and flattered by his compliment in spite of her harsh words to him. "You'll get very tired of it before a week, with just the two of us. I hope you brought a good book to read."

"On my honeymoon—never! There'll be plenty to do that you'll like. You'll see. Trust me, you won't need a book," he said, nuzzling her neck, while his hand drifted along her arm.

She closed her eyes, relishing the sensations he caused, knowing if they got beyond just kisses, she would forget her surroundings and all thoughts of waiting until later for lovemaking.

A pang of wishful thinking rocked her while she caressed his nape. If only they were wildly in love how different this day and tonight would be! She opened her eyes to run her fingers through his thick hair as he pressed sultry kisses on her throat.

She wanted his love instead of this impetuous union where sex and the baby were the big ties for Ryan. She inhaled, closed her eyes and tried to stop thinking about the absence of his love.

Finally, gulping for air, she scooted off his lap to another seat while she straightened her clothing. She looked up to find him studying her with a scalding look that blatantly undressed her.

"Slow down, Ryan. Your kisses are melting me and we're not alone up here. We wait until we're in the hotel room in Houston."

"I'll be patient, but I don't want to," he said in a husky voice she barely recognized.

They landed in bright sunshine and drove to the hotel. Soon Ryan was opening the door to a suite on the top floor. He picked her up to carry her inside. "Now we really begin our lives together as Mr. and Mrs. Ryan Warner," he said.

Eight

Solemnly, she wrapped her arm around his neck. Everything they did made her long for a deep, binding love between them. Reminding herself to be thankful for what he was giving her—marriage to him, his name, financial support forever for their baby—she tried to cling to positives.

As he carried her over the threshold and closed the door behind them, she had a momentary glimpse of a spacious room furnished in white and pale blue, with elegant fruitwood furniture and a balcony beyond glass doors. A huge bouquet of gerbera daises and orange tiger lilies in a crystal vase stood on a low table. Sparkling cider was already on ice, ordered in advance by Ryan.

Closing the door, he set her on her feet and slid one arm around her waist, drawing her against him.

Her husband. Mrs. Ryan Warner. How long would it take for her to accept it?

"We're starting life together and I expect it to be fabulous," he said quietly.

She placed her hand on Ryan's cheek. "I told you, I'll make you fall in love with me."

"I'd say we're headed in that direction. You can't imagine how much I want you right now," he said, his voice hoarse.

"I want more, Ryan. I want your heart, your love, your total commitment to our relationship," she said. She was his wife now and would be with him. So much was up to her—whether she turned him away or seduced him into a binding love....

Holding her close, he bent his head to kiss her. She pressed against him, aching for all of his marvelous body. She pushed away his coat. His fingers were on the buttons of her dress, but she was barely aware because his kisses were stoking her passion. Memories crashed over her of the taste and texture of him.

He leaned back, releasing her for a moment to unfasten his collar and remove his tie. His scalding stare locked with hers as he reached out to draw her dress off her shoulders.

Pushing it away, he let it slide down over her hips, following it with his eyes and making every inch of her tingle. She wore only her lacy white wisp of a bra and a skimpy thong.

"Damn, you're beautiful," he whispered, his voice a rasp. He reached out to peel away her bra.

His breathing was already ragged from their kisses, and the power she held over him—physically—amazed her, exciting her in turn, fueling her hopes of binding his heart to her forever.

His longing fused with her yearning. She was as surprised by the depth of her own desire for him, a need that had tormented her on too many empty nights.

Wanting to touch his bare warm skin and to look at him as freely as he gazed at her, she reached for him, unfastening the studs of his shirt and tugging the tails out of his pants. She caressed his broad, muscular chest, tangling her fingers in his thick, black curls and then letting her fingers range over his washboard belly. He was solid, all muscles, lean and hard. Irresistible. Drawing her to him, he enveloped her in his arms and kissed her with even more hunger than before.

Wanting him, she burned, moving her hips and moaning softly while his hands slipped down to cup her breasts and caress her.

"I intend to pleasure you all night," he whispered, while his thumbs circled her nipples. Her memories had not been exaggerations; he was the lover she'd recalled. Hot, exciting, deliberate and provoking. He might be even better this time, because he seemed driven. She held his hips, gasping and closing her eyes. He leaned down to tease each taut nipple with his tongue in wet, lazy circles that sent sensations to her core.

She unfastened his trousers and he stepped out of them, yanking off his socks and tossing them away. He was aroused, thick and ready, and she hooked her fingers in his briefs to peel them down. She came up slowly, running her hands along his legs, trailing her tongue over him, looking at his spectacular body, his thick rod, which was throbbing for her now.

He caught her to lift her up into his embrace. Thrilling to everything he did, she locked her arms around his neck and nuzzled him, letting go of all her anger.

They kissed with mutual heat, hearts thudding. She could feel his pounding heart beneath her fingers as she caressed his chest. She knew his need was escalating as swiftly as hers. She wanted her husband and she hoped to seduce him as much as he enticed her.

In the bedroom, he set her on her feet and yanked away the covering on the bed. She was oblivious to their surroundings, seeing only the virile, naked man standing before her. She reached for him, grasping his slender hips, and then her hands played over him and slid around to his firm buttocks. She knelt, exploring his muscled thighs while she traced her tongue across his belly and heard his deep intake of breath.

Her fingers found his shaft, thick and hard, and she stroked him before she took him into her mouth. Her tongue circled the velvet tip as she remembered the textures of him, learned what excited him most, discovered more about his responses.

Making a sound deep in his throat, he slipped his hands beneath her arms and hauled her to her feet, and his scalding look was as evocative as a kiss.

"You're the woman of my dreams and fantasies," he rasped in a deep voice, making her wonder if he meant what he said or was lost in passion. Kissing her, he drew her into his embrace, holding her with one arm while his other hand slid down to caress her.

Moaning, she burned with need for him. Her cries were taken by his mouth on hers. His shaft was hard against her belly, a reinforcement of what he'd told her. He leaned away to look at her. "I want to make love to you until you let me do everything to pleasure you. I know how passionate you can be, and memories of our lovemaking have tormented me night after night. This is a sweet revenge for those sleepless hours," he whispered, leaning down for another fiery kiss.

Ashley caught his firm jaw in her hand. "You're not the only one seeking retaliation for haunting nights alone, with memories of loving that made sleep impossible. Sweet revenge is two-way, Ryan," she added softly. "I hope to drive you to lose that control you always have, that super-charged assurance you exhibit to the world. I intend to love you into a frenzy of need, and bind your heart to mine so you'll fall in love with me forever."

His eyes darkened and his face flushed with heat as he pulled her roughly to him, stopping her words with his mouth and ending any thoughts that made her doubt his need. He leaned over her until she had to cling to him tightly.

When he swung her into his arms, his body was hot against hers. With care, he lowered her to the bed, then knelt beside her. Starting at her ankles, he took his time caressing her, his stormy gaze consuming her all the while.

While he inched slowly up her legs, his tongue and his warm hands played over her. Her eyes were squeezed shut tightly as her hips moved and she opened herself to him.

He moved higher across her belly, then lavished attention on each breast, stroking them with his tongue. When she thought she couldn't stand one more minute, he turned her over on her belly and began caressing her nape and buttocks, working his way down again. When he kissed and teased the backs of her knees, she came up on the bed with a cry and pushed him down, to kiss and explore his body, wanting to drive him over the same edge.

After showering kisses on his inner thighs, she licked his hard shaft. He sat up, taking her in his embrace and silencing her protest that she had just started to explore him.

He held her in his arms, kissing her and shifting her until they were stretched out, and his hand went between her legs to rub and heighten her need, already at a fever pitch. Her pulse drummed in an escalating rhythm.

"Ryan!" she gasped as his fingers tormented her, driving her to want even more. And then he shifted again, spreading her thighs and moving between them, hooking her legs over his broad, strong shoulders to give him full access to her.

He leaned closer to kiss her, his tongue stroking her feminine bud, a new torment that consumed her until she writhed and shifted.

Once, she opened her eyes and saw he was watching her. "Ryan!" she moaned, holding his shaft and letting her hand play between his thighs.

She was incredibly sensual and enticing, and he thought he might burst with need for her, but he fought for control. He wanted to pleasure her until she was wild.

His gaze ran over her full breasts and pale, lush body. She had no idea what she did to him. Having her long legs over his shoulders had taken his iron control almost to a breaking point. And the honeyed essence of her, open to him, vulnerable, yet able to consume him whole, was driving him wild. She could never imagine the depth of his longing for her.

He watched her as he kissed and teased her, his own responses building with lightning speed until he knew his control wouldn't last much longer. But he wanted to take her slowly. Her pleasure fueled his, and was top priority.

She cried out for him, while her hips moved until he had to have her. He shifted her legs off his shoulders and lowered himself, knowing that now he no longer had to use protection.

As her eyes flew open, she came up to wrap her arms around him and kiss him, her tongue driving him to another brink, until he pushed her back on the bed. He lowered himself again, his shaft touching her softness, brushing her, teasing, until he entered her slowly, all the while fighting to hold back.

Instantly responsive, she arched to meet him, tugging

him to her, enveloping him in her softness. Her long legs locked tightly around him. Crying out while her hips arched, she grasped his buttocks and her head thrashed.

Sweat poured off him. Hot, seductive, she was the fulfillment of his dreams. He struggled to take his time with her.

"Ashley." He ground out her name, wanting her. "Ashley."

Ashley barely heard her name, with her pulse thundering so. Every inch of her was on fire with his loving.

He filled her deeply, moving slowly, a sweet torment that continued to build until finally his thrusts became swift and desperate, rising to a pounding rhythm.

Lights exploded behind her closed eyes. Groaning, she raised slightly to nip at his shoulder and neck, raking her fingers over his back and his buttocks.

They rocked together, physical need intensifying until she climaxed in an explosive release that caused tremors to shake her.

"Ryan! Oh, Ryan!"

"Darlin' Ashley," he whispered hoarsely in return, thrusting swiftly, pleasuring her beyond her wildest dreams.

He was hard, full, evoking sensation after sensation as he climaxed and shuddered, and still continued to thrust deeply, carrying her to another swift climax that engulfed her in rapture.

"You're mine," she whispered, knowing that in the throes of loving, he wouldn't hear her. Nor would it matter if he did. For this moment, he was hers, heart and body.

Ecstasy swamped her. Sight, thought, hearing all diminished, leaving her in a whirlwind of sensation and giving her a sense of closeness to the man in her arms.

Joined as one now, she moved with him, wanting to hold this moment as tightly as she held him, and hoping to bind him to her in love as much as they were bound by lust.

Eagerly, she ran her hands over him while she basked in their intimacy. It was a momentary triumph, one she knew was fleeting. Yet tonight, he had been hers entirely, desiring her to an extent she wouldn't have dreamed possible. Their lovemaking validated the possibility of love between them someday.

As he lowered his weight, she held him tightly. They were wet with perspiration, satiated, wrapped in each other and euphoria. He turned his head to place kisses on her cheek and the corner of her mouth. She kissed him in return. Even though she knew this joy was temporary, she relished it.

Rolling to his side, he kept her with him, holding her close. She could feel his heart, still pumping as hard and fast as hers. While the rhythm gradually slowed, and their breathing became regular, she stroked his back. He gazed at her with pleasure, smoothing long locks of damp hair from her face and tucking them behind her ear.

"We're off to a grand start, Ashley."

"I agree with you on that one," she said, and he smiled.

"Such reluctance to say I'm right!" he remarked with amusement.

She placed her finger on his lips. "Shh. No reality for now. I want to enjoy this moment."

"This is real, believe me. If you don't think so, I'll show you," he whispered. He traced the curve of her ear with his tongue and his warm breath on her ear tickled her. She inhaled as excitement bubbled again.

"Ryan!"

He arched one dark eyebrow. "See? Loving is real and I'm real."

"I know you are," she said, smiling at him, refusing to let anything intrude on the joy enveloping her.

"Ah, Ashley, it's hot between us. Better now than the last

time we were together, and that was so fabulous I didn't think it could be topped. You're an alluring woman, delicious and seductive."

She nuzzled his neck and moved sensuously against him. "I hope you think so."

"You're starting something."

"Not at all. I didn't do anything except stretch a little. Like this," she said, rubbing him with her body again, and he inhaled deeply. "There's someone else in this bed who is sizzling and seductive," she said softly.

"That does it," he replied, shifting until she could feel his rod, thick and hard once more. Wrapping his arm around her waist, he kissed her.

To her surprise, desire rocked her, when a few minutes earlier she hadn't thought she would feel that way for hours. Yet she remembered from before how he abounded with energy and stamina, enabling him to make love for hours. An answering urgency drove her to push him down and straddle him.

He gazed at her with hooded eyes as he clasped her hips and impaled her on his thick shaft. Gasping, she closed her eyes in ecstasy while he caressed between her thighs, and his other hand toyed with her nipples.

Once again, passion rocked her as she moved her hips, meeting his hard thrusts. When her climax burst with the same force as before, Ryan shuddered with his.

With a cry she tumbled onto him, limp, covered in perspiration, exhausted once again, yet as fulfilled as before.

He wrapped his arms around her and held her. His heart still pounded with hers.

"You've exhausted me," she said softly. "I can't move."

His arm tightened around her. "I don't want you to move. I want you part of me," he said gruffly.

Thrilled by his declaration, she lay still and ran her fingers along his arm, feeling the bulge of muscles even when he was doing nothing. "You're strong, Ryan."

"And you're seductive," he replied. "Sensual, absolute temptation!"

"You say one more adjective and I won't believe any of them."

"Nope. That's all I had to say," he replied. "Shortly, we'll shower. And when you want dinner sent up, you tell me. I long for only one thing," he insisted.

"What a one-track mind you have!" she exclaimed, and rose up on her arms to look down at him. His gaze lowered to her bare breasts and he cupped them in his large, tanned hands, rubbing his thumbs lightly over her nipples.

"This is why I have a one-track mind," he said with that rasp in his voice he always had when he was excited. He pulled her forward to draw his tongue across her nipples.

"Ryan! We just loved! You can't—"

"Oh, yes, I can, when I look at you like this," he said, nuzzling her and then taking her nipple in his mouth.

Closing her eyes, she inhaled and moaned as pleasure shot deep inside, heating her yet again. She shifted beside him and he rolled over to wrap his arm around her and kiss her.

This time his lovemaking was as intense as before, yet more deliberate, until finally they climaxed and once again held each other. Ashley was enveloped in bliss. "I thought we set a world record that weekend we met, but this weekend, if it keeps up—"

"It will be up, thanks to you," he remarked lazily, and she laughed. "Craving you as I do, we'll surpass that weekend, I promise. You didn't know how much I meant it when I said I wanted you more than you could possibly imagine."

"I don't recall you telling me any such thing."

"You don't pay attention. I did tell you," he said, holding her close in the curve of his arm.

She sat up, pulling the sheet under her arms.

He played with locks of her hair, his warm hand brushing her bare back. "What are you doing?" he asked with amusement.

"Looking around at where we are. I didn't notice the place when we came in. This is lovely."

"It *is* lovely," he repeated, in a voice that indicated his thoughts were on her instead of their surroundings. She glanced down at him.

"From your tone I know you weren't referring to the hotel. While I have the chance, I'm grabbing my shower."

Beneath his steady gaze, she stepped out of bed. "Ryan, stop watching me that way!" she exclaimed. "You're making me blush."

"You're making me hot and bothered," he drawled, putting his hands behind his head and letting his gaze drift over her again.

She tried to pull the sheet from the king-size bed and wrap it around her, but it was too firmly tucked in. It held, pulling tightly just above her knees as she tugged at it. He laughed and came out of bed, yanking away the sheet and ignoring her cry of protest.

He picked her up and headed to the shower. "We'll do this together."

"And I can imagine what that'll lead to."

"Tell me. What?"

"You know as well as I do."

"I want to hear you say it and talk about loving again. It's a turn-on."

"You don't need any turn-on. You're inflamed without me doing anything."

"You're doing plenty. Looking ravishing, seductive and naked. Responding to my slightest touch. Touching me in ways that would fry any man."

"If you keep talking, we'll never make it to the shower," she said, nuzzling his neck.

"Yes, we will," he replied. Carrying her into the large glass shower, he set her on her feet and turned on the warm water. As she ran her hands over his sleek, firm body, he drew a washcloth across her nipples, rubbing gently to arouse her.

She tingled, heat pooling within her while she caressed him in return, sliding her hands over his strong shoulders, slipping them down his hips and his belly. Dropping the washcloth, he leaned forward to kiss her.

His warm, wet body excited her, yet when he held her away to look at her, she knew the sight of her stirred him in turn. Water poured over them as he took his time.

Strong and virile, he was perfection. His black hair was plastered to his head, some locks on his forehead giving him a more dangerous look. Married only hours, acquainted less than a year, she wondered what risks they took, knowing each other so little. Added to that was his ruthless, arrogant streak… Yet his charm and irresistible sex appeal offset his strong will.

Could she keep him from breaking her heart? Or entice him to fall in love with her? Questions with no answers plagued her. One thing was certain: she loved him.

Ryan's hands slid over her and electrified her. She trembled with his touch, while her need built as insistently as before.

His hand slid along the inside of her thigh and up her belly, higher until he cupped her breasts, while his leg thrust between hers. He circled her waist with his arm, pulling her close against him, raising his leg to put pressure against her feminine bud.

"Ryan—"

He kissed away her words.

As she rubbed against his leg, she caressed him. She had her eyes closed, relishing all the sensations. Warm water splashed over them and heat built to an inferno.

He picked her up and spread his legs to brace himself, while she wrapped around him. He settled her on his thick rod, letting her slide down so he could fill her.

She cried out with pleasure and leaned forward to nip his shoulder lightly and then kiss him. Her heart pounded as he thrust into her softness, filling her, driving her to release.

"Ryan, love me!" she cried, holding him tightly while she kissed him again. She felt his climax come with hers, and then they slowed, until finally, she lowered her legs once again.

"You've exhausted me," she said, smiling up at him and stroking his jaw. "Now let me shower."

"Of course. That's why we're in here together."

She gave him a rueful, teasing look. "I'm sure a shower is all you had in mind when you carried me in here."

He chuckled. "Admit it. Was that the best shower you've ever had or not? And I know what answer I better hear."

She leaned closer and placed her hand over her heart. "My darlin', it was definitely the sexiest shower ever," she drawled, and he grinned.

"I had to wring that one from you."

"You certainly did," she said haughtily, turning her back on him to step out of the shower. He gave her a playful swat on the bottom.

"Hey!" she said, but she was teasing as much as he was.

"Let me kiss it and make it well."

"Don't you dare! I'm getting out of this shower and drying before my skin wrinkles up and I look like a prune."

"Darlin', you couldn't look like a prune if you stood under water until tomorrow."

"Thank you, but I'd feel like one." When she grabbed a fluffy towel to dry off, he took it from her hands.

"Let me do this," he commanded.

"Thank you, kind sir," she said politely, and he rubbed her languidly while he watched her.

Desire ignited yet again, startling her at how easily he could do that to her. And then he carried her to the bed to love her again.

It was well past four in the morning when they showered once more and she insisted on drying herself. "I'm starving, Ryan. I was too excited and nervous to eat before the wedding, too busy to eat during it, and we've been making love since."

"I'll have something sent up."

"At this hour?"

"Yep. A small crew stays until four in the morning. The morning crew arrives at five, so we give service all through the night. So do I," he added in a deep voice.

"I see that gleam in your eye. Wait until we at least order."

"And then I can have my way with you?"

"Actually, wait until we eat. If you kiss me, I'll never hear a knock, and I'll miss my dinner."

"Would you care?" he asked playfully.

"My stomach would, but you know what you do to me. You can make me forget the world."

He dropped his towel and walked over to take her shoulders in his hands, peering at her searchingly. "I hope I can. And I hope I always do."

She focused more intently on him, hearing a uncustomary, solemn note in his voice. "You know you do. You're doing it right now."

He leaned down to kiss her hard, pulling her tightly against him. She didn't know how long they kissed, but he was flushed when he released her.

"I'll wait and feed you. I don't want you to faint from hunger."

"If you'll catch me, I don't mind," she said.

"I'll always catch you. Keep me around and you're safe."

"I hope so," she answered solemnly, thinking they both were referring to different facets of their lives, making promises to each other that she wondered whether either one of them would keep. "I hope you don't break my heart," she repeated.

"Never, Ashley. You'll see. I keep my word."

Again she could hear Kayla's warning—that he wouldn't be faithful to one woman. Carefully, Ashley wrapped a towel around herself.

He yanked up a clean one and knotted it around his waist, going to get a menu, which he held out to her. "Look and see what you want. I know what *I* want," he added in a husky voice, looking at her breasts.

"Ryan, stop coming on to me for just a few minutes while we get some food."

"I'll try, but you're making it difficult."

She inhaled and with an effort opened the elegant, embossed red menu to search for what sounded tasty. "Think I can order any of this at this time of night?"

"Tell me what you want and I'll ask. There's a restaurant around the corner that's open all night, so they can go there and get what you want if they don't have it here."

"I'd like the baked chicken," she said, and handed him the menu. She left him to go blow-dry her hair.

Within the hour they sat at a dining table with food spread before them. Both were dressed in thick, dark blue robes furnished by the hotel.

They removed the covers from their dishes and she looked at the golden baked chicken and the steaming baked potato she had ordered. "I'm starving, Ryan," she said, sipping her water and then cutting into the chicken.

Ryan had a thick, juicy steak and baked potato. After a couple of bites, she looked up to find him watching her with a steady, smoldering gaze.

"What?" she asked.

"I'm thinking about us and our future. We can start planning the house we want to build, and when we return home, pick out where you want to live."

She thought about Dallas and the possibilities. "I want one near the schools where we'll send our baby."

He nodded. "I agree, but you might consider private schools because we can afford it."

"When there's a grandchild, my family will want to see us often, and your dad may want to, too. He's right there in Dallas, so it'll be easy with him," she said, mulling over possibilities. "It might help to live in a suburb on the northeast."

"That's fine with me. Whatever you want. We'll have to pick a name. It's too early to have an ultrasound and know what you're having, isn't it?"

"Yes, it is," she said. "Do you care whether it's a boy or a girl?"

He shook his head. "No. Maybe I hope slightly for a girl, because I grew up in a house of males, but I don't mind if we don't get one. Just a healthy baby."

"I agree, but I'm glad to know that's the way you feel."

"Aah, so we're in complete harmony on this issue, too."

"What else have we been in complete harmony about?" she asked in amusement.

He glanced beyond her and pointed, and she looked over her shoulder into the empty bedroom to a bed with tangled covers. "Oh, so we have," she said, turning to smile at him.

His green eyes had darkened and she knew he had forgotten food.

"Have you eaten enough yet to keep from fainting or getting sick?"

"Yes," she said, barely able to speak as she watched him get up and come around to take her hand. Her heart raced and she forgot all about her dinner, seeing only the tall, handsome man who was now her husband.

He wrapped his arms around her and kissed her. The minute he touched her, her heart thudded.

She locked her arms around him to return his kisses. Soon he pushed away her robe and shed his, kissing her as he picked her up to carry her back to the bedroom.

She was amazed that they made love continually through the rest of the early morning. They dozed finally, long after sunlight spilled into the bedroom. She woke to open her eyes and look at Ryan while he slept.

They were locked in each other's arms. His dark lashes were feathery shadows on his cheeks. Black stubble showed on his unshaved jaw. She wondered if she would ever tire of looking at him, just as he had said about gazing at her.

His eyes opened. He was instantly awake and she was ensnared in depths of green.

"Good morning, Mrs. Warner. Today will be the first full day of our marriage. Let's make it as good as it can possibly be. I seem to recall something about promising no physical relationship, but can I have a few hugs and kisses and loving this morning, because it's still part of our wedding night?"

Nine

Without answering, she gazed at him. Her pulse raced. She could feel his thick shaft, hard and hot, pressed against her. She didn't feel like talking, and her longing for him was intense.

Those locks of black hair fell over his brow again. Pushing them away, she looked at his mouth. She slid her hand behind his head and drew him to her, to place her lips on his and kiss him.

Instantly, his arm banded her waist and he pulled her tightly against him. He shifted them, rolling her over on her back as he moved on top of her.

She had given him an answer with her actions, yet when would they go back to life without a physical relationship? Did she even want to, now?

He kissed her, turning slightly so he could caress her breast, moving her legs apart with his, and then slid into her, filling her while she cried out with pleasure.

After release came for her, and he climaxed, he held her close beside him and once again lay facing her.

"Good morning, Mrs. Warner. What a fantastic way to start our day."

"We agree there, too. Right now, I don't want to move. This is paradise."

"Then don't move," he replied. "We can stay right here for hours or all day or until tomorrow. Whatever you want."

She smiled at him. "We're off to a great beginning," she said, tracing his lips with her index finger, until he caught it in his teeth and licked the tip lightly. "Can you stop being sexy for just one minute and let me catch my breath?"

"I think that's my question to you. I'm just reacting to you."

She felt happy, pushing away worries or memories that she knew would take away her peace. "What's the program today?"

"To make love to you."

"Not all day!" she exclaimed, laughing. "And where did that promise go to wait for a physical relationship?"

"That's up to you. Is that what you still want?" he asked, gazing at her intently with a solemn expression.

As she pondered their future, she drew her finger along his jaw. Should they rush into a sexual, lusty relationship that would evaporate when they had a crisis? Or would it bind them together? She couldn't answer her own questions. "This is good, Ryan," she said.

"It's more than good. It's fabulous, spectacular sex."

What they had so far had been awesome. Why take that away? "Let's put that decision off until after the honeymoon," she answered carefully. "What do you think about that?"

"You don't have to ask twice," he said with a flare of unmistakable satisfaction in his eyes.

"But," she said, placing her hand against his chest as he

started to lean closer to kiss her. "I want to eat breakfast or my cold dinner or something. You know we only ate about four bites last night."

"You're right. My stomach is complaining, and it's not good for you to miss meals. Let's forget that cold dinner and have breakfast."

"Super!" she exclaimed, starting to get up. But he caught her wrist.

"Stay where you are. I'll get the menus and we can read them in bed and order from here."

"That sound suspiciously like you have other intentions."

"Not at all," he said with great innocence. "Except there may be a little time between ordering and delivery of our breakfasts for me to get in a kiss or two."

She laughed and settled against the pillow. "Get the menus."

He climbed out of bed and crossed the room. He was nude, muscular and fit, and she relished looking at him. To her surprise, passion flared again. She was amazed how easily he could get her excited. He disappeared into the other room and in minutes returned.

Again, he was ready for love, and when he reached the bed, he stood beside her, offering her a menu.

She touched him, stroking him lightly. "You're awake again."

"That's because of you, but we order first. I really don't want you sick this morning, or fainting or going hungry."

"Then you better get under the sheet and out of my sight," she whispered, sitting up to flick her tongue over him. He gasped, but moved away, going around the bed and slipping beneath the sheet to sit close beside her and pull her into his arms.

By the time their breakfasts arrived, they had made love

again and showered and dressed in the blue robes. She stayed in the bedroom while Ryan dealt with the break-fast delivery and removal of their early morning dinner. Finally he came to get her, taking her hand, and they ate on the balcony.

A faint breeze toyed with his hair as he smiled at her and reached across the table to hold her hand. "I planned for us to fly out of here at eleven this morning," he said.

"I don't have any idea what time it is now," she said.

"It's around nine."

"Great heavens! Don't we have to leave soon? We have to be at the airport about two hours early if we have an international flight."

"Not if it's my jet. Eleven is when I told my pilot we'd leave. We have time, and I'll keep my eye on the clock."

"I'm lost in a world that's just you and paradise," she said.

As his eyes darkened, he squeezed her hand lightly. "Later, I'll show you how much your statement means to me."

"Not yet," she replied. "I have to eat breakfast."

While Ashley gazed at the patio and hotel grounds spread out below, Ryan absorbed her profile, looking at her long lashes and flawless skin, which was soft as rose petals. His attention shifted to her full lips, so delicate, yet so easily inflamed when pressed against his.

He was getting aroused, desiring her again, wondering if he would ever reach the point where he could study her mouth, think about her kisses, without becoming excited. He ached for more sex with her, and he intended to seduce her all over again, if possible, because it would be a living hell to be with her and unable to make love to her.

With every second they were together, their marriage seemed a better idea. How could she continually resist this union between them? He could give her so much, and he longed to share his life with her and with their baby.

She turned her head to gaze at him, and he was riveted by her crystal blue eyes, certain he had married the most beautiful, enticing woman possible.

"What are you thinking, Ryan? Although I'm not sure I need to ask…"

Looking at her pale, slender fingers, he lifted her hand to his mouth to brush kisses across her knuckles. "I'm desiring you, admiring you, aching for you, remembering last night and this morning, wanting to pull you into my lap and remove that robe and let you take me to paradise."

"I believe we have a flight to catch, and you're not doing any such thing out here on this balcony." She looked away. "It's the most gorgeous morning. This view is wonderful."

"It's more wonderful in the bedroom," he said in a low tone that revealed his arousal.

She turned to look at him, and the fire in her eyes made him miss a breath. "Then why don't we go in there?" she asked in a sultry voice, and his temperature jumped.

He stood, holding her hand while they went inside, stopping in front of the long mirrors that covered one wall. Turning her to face him, he reached down to catch the end of the tie around her waist. He drew it loose and released it. While he watched her, he pushed open her robe.

She was naked beneath it, and she closed her eyes when he peeled it away. His hands went to her waist, and he was on fire while he took his time, letting his gaze drift over her, and then looking into the mirror to see her back and tiny waist, narrow bottom and long, shapely legs. He turned her around and pulled her up against him, playing with her breasts.

"Look at us, Ashley. You're gorgeous and this is awesome."

With one glance, she twisted back around to wrap her arms around him and kiss him, and he held her, fighting to keep control so he could take time to love her.

Later, when their chartered plane was airborne, circling and turning south, Ashley gazed below at the blue Gulf. When Ryan took her hand, she glanced at him.

"How can you sit there and not look at this marvelous view?"

When he shrugged, she wrinkled her nose at him. "Jaded traveler," she accused, and turned back to the window.

"I hope you like it," he said, leaning close to nuzzle her neck. "I hope to show you the world. And we'll show our baby, too."

When she studied him with a searching stare, his dark eyebrows arched. "What's that look mean?"

"You surprise me continually," she said quietly. "I never know what to expect from you."

"Good. That adds some spice and interest to life. I'd hate to hear you say I'm completely predictable."

"I'd like to be able to predict a few things and to understand you."

"It'll take a lifetime, I hope, for us to explore each other's facets."

"You are an optimist, self-assured, cavalier and determined."

"Aah," he said, kissing her throat and then raising his head to look into her eyes. "With the exception of arrogant, we're alike in all of those qualities, except perhaps you're not quite the optimist I am."

"Oh, please! There is no way I'm as arrogant and strong willed."

"I hope the day will come that you'll say, 'Darlin', you

were right, and what you did was wonderful for all of us,'"
he said, caressing her nape and making her forget their
conversation.

"You stop being irresistible for a little while!"

"Now who's being determined and strong willed?" he
asked with a twinkle in his eyes.

"We can't make love here on this plane," she insisted.

"It's mine and we can, but we won't if you want to wait."

She turned back to look below, and saw a vast stretch
of blue water that met blue sky in the distance.

It was afternoon when he carried her across another
threshold, into his villa. He walked straight through to the
bedroom, which opened out onto a patio and beyond it to
white sand and blue waters, with frothy white breakers lap-
ping the shore.

"Ryan, this is paradise!" she exclaimed, thinking it the
most breathtaking place she'd ever seen.

"I intend for it to be," he said, and set her on her feet
and stepped away. "This is where we'll be for our honeymoon. The servants have already left for today, and there
are only three on duty now. Two of them cook and one
cleans. They're leaving us stocked with food, and they'll
come in a couple of days to replenish what's needed. You'll
meet them when they arrive. There's not another place for
several miles in either direction, so we'll have privacy. But
we can go into town if we want to."

Barely listening, she reached out to take his hand and
pull him toward her. The minute she tugged lightly, he
stopped talking, focusing on her as she wrapped her arms
around his neck to kiss him.

Instantly, he embraced her. She had seen the flash of
surprise in his expression, but it was gone as swiftly as it
had come. Kissing her deeply, he leaned over her.

In seconds they were in a frenzy of loving, as if he were determined to bind her to him. In the throes of passion, they moved wildly together. Squeezing her eyes closed tightly, Ashley held Ryan. Her thoughts spun away, lost to the urgency of the moment, yet she turned her head, unable to hold back.

"I love you," she barely whispered. Her heart was hopelessly Ryan's, forever.

Later, when she lay naked, spent and blissful in his arms, he trailed kisses on her cheek and stroked her hair from her face. He rose up on one elbow to look down at her. "Ashley, it just gets more and more fantastic between us. The more I make love to you, the more I want you."

Solemnly, she gazed up at him, brushing raven locks off his forehead. "That's ridiculous, but I'm happy to hear you say it," she said, wondering if he'd heard her whisper her love for him. He hadn't, she decided. Ryan wouldn't let such a declaration pass unheeded. What if she told him now?

She stroked her hand over his shoulder as he nuzzled her throat. He'd made no such commitment to her. Even in the most intense moments between them, there were no words of love.

If she revealed her feelings for him, would he declare love for her out of a sense of obligation, or in an attempt to please her? She didn't think he would. She suspected he would never say the words unless he meant them.

When she brushed a kiss on his cheek, he looked at her with obvious happiness. He'd accused her of being strong willed, independent and confident, but she wasn't where he was concerned. He had gotten past the barriers around her heart, overcome her cool logic and burned away her resistance with his kisses.

"This intimacy between us will bring us closer together," he said. "You'll see."

"I hope you're right," she answered, rubbing her leg
along his and causing him to take a long breath.

"I thought you'd want to swim," he remarked in a
husky voice.

"I do, and we can as soon as we shower," she said, rolling away from him.

He pulled her back. "You just indicated you wanted
something else," he said gruffly.

"Because of this?" she asked, rubbing her leg against
him again, and his eyes darkened.

He pulled her close to kiss her. "The swim can wait,"
he said. "I can't."

The last day of their honeymoon, the first Saturday in
May, was spent leisurely swimming, breakfasting on the
patio, making love and then swimming again. Over lunch,
Ashley took Ryan's hand, to rub her thumb lightly over
his knuckles.

"Soon we go back to work and schedules and travel. I
have a wedding in Houston as soon as we return, and I'll
be gone at least four nights."

"I have to go to San Diego for a hotel opening, so I'll
be away, too. I'll get back on Friday. We'll celebrate our
reunion," he said, smiling at her.

"I won't get home until Saturday night, so you'll have
a night alone."

"And they can't move the wedding up a day because of
your poor, lonely husband?" he joked. She wrinkled her
nose at him. "You know how difficult that would be! You
know that much about weddings."

"I won't like you being in Houston longer than I'll be

gone, but it'll make it all the greater when you arrive. We'll have a spectacular homecoming."

"Ryan, this week has been fabulous! You've entertained me, made endless, fantastic love to me, showered me with gifts and fed me exotic, delicious food. Every minute with you has been pure bliss. I hate to leave paradise and go back to reality," she admitted.

He smiled and raised her hand, pressing the back of it against his cheek. "I'll do everything I can to make it great for you at home," he said. "As for me, all you have to do is be there and it's paradise."

Her heart missed a beat and she stared at him, thinking that was as close to any admission of strong feelings for her that he had made.

"I think the friendship between us is growing, Ashley," he said with a firm tone of voice. "We've talked for hours this week and learned a lot about each other, what we like and what we want. We've done things together and had fabulous times. You've told me some problems you're having with approaching weddings and I've made some suggestions. I've told you about some of my difficulties and dislikes in my business, how I hate traveling a lot and you've made suggestions that are valid."

"You have, Ryan, and you're right about all of what you just said. We're getting closer," she said, filled with joy over what he'd admitted.

"Your suggestion to consolidate two of my offices makes me wonder why I didn't think of it. I can count on you and confide in you, and I hope you feel that way with me. And although I had to talk you into our marriage, I still dream the day will come when you'll tell me you're glad I got you into this union."

Her hope soared that he was falling in love. She thrilled

to his admission, which was another strong indication that he was committing himself to her in a permanent relationship, and that it was important to him.

"Ryan, your declarations mean more to me than I can ever tell you," she whispered, going around the small table to sit in his lap.

He pulled her close and kissed her, and conversation ended. But she knew she would never forget a word he had said to her.

Later in the day, when they were packed and ready to leave, and the car had come for them, Ashley paused to look around. She could hear the small breakers along the beach. Through the open doors she saw the bed where they'd shared such fabulous lovemaking.

"We'll be back, Ashley," Ryan said, watching her. "This is my place, after all."

"I know, but this was our honeymoon, a once-in-a-lifetime experience, and it was truly paradise." She turned to look up at him. "Every moment of it was wonderful, Ryan," she said sincerely, surprised how much the week had meant to her. Would the day arrive when she'd admit to him that he'd been right to bribe her into this marriage? She couldn't imagine she would ever agree with his high-handed ways, even if she was thoroughly happy and thankful to be married to him.

He dropped the bag he was holding and crossed the last bit of space between them, to take her into his arms and kiss her hard and long, until she placed her hand against his shoulder and wriggled. "Ryan! The car is waiting!"

He grinned and picked up his briefcase, while a man approached the house to take the luggage.

In the car, she glanced back, enjoying the sight of his

sprawling villa, thinking it would always be paradise on earth to her. Ryan draped his arm across her shoulders and pulled her close as they sped to the airport and his private jet.

"We'll start right away if you feel like it, looking for property for the house we'll build. You can tell me what decorator you want. I have a builder, unless you have any objection."

"None," she replied. "I don't know any builders."

"Good. I'll get my secretary to gather information about schools. When we have an idea where we'd like to live, we can investigate the school situation more thoroughly."

"I'll check into schools, too, Ryan. I think it will be more important to learn about them first. Let's find an excellent school and then see if we like the area."

"That's reasonable," he agreed, and she smiled.

"It'll take a while to build a house, so get your decorator and let's put a nursery in my condo," he added. "I have plenty of room. That way we won't have to be in a rush to move or build, and we can do it all when you feel like it."

"Wonderful!" she exclaimed. "I couldn't deal with a big move right now."

"I'm glad you told me, and that you always let me know how you feel."

"I will. When have I not voiced my objections?"

He laughed. "As far as I'm aware, you've let them be known with me."

"I'll continue to do so. If you don't like it, that's tough, because you brought all this on yourself," she said in a haughty tone, and he grinned.

When they arrived at his condo, and Ryan picked her up to carry her inside, she laughed. "How many times are you carrying me over a threshold?"

"As many times as possible. I like having you in my arms, and you're a featherweight."

"Hardly, but I'm happy about it," she said, locking both arms around his neck. They went inside and he kicked the door closed behind him, then set her on her feet.

"Welcome home," he said warmly, and she smiled. "Ryan, this marriage is good. I'll admit that so far, I love being married to you."

"So far? I'm going to have to do better. I want unconditional acceptance."

She almost added, "I want your love," but she bit back the words and hugged him instead, before he could detect the depth of her feelings for him. He was far too perceptive, and she was amazed he hadn't realized before now that she loved him.

"What you're getting is back to routines and schedules and problems," she said. "We both are."

"I'll always come home to you, and that'll make it all worth it."

Always. Once again his statement spoke of a developing bond between them, and she prayed that's what was happening, because her love for him was increasing daily. It wouldn't be long before he was going to realize her true feelings. She kissed him, holding him, wanting him to stop studying her. She didn't want him to have the even greater advantage of knowing she loved him. She suspected arguments over the baby still lay ahead, and she'd learned the hard way that Ryan would latch on to any advantage to get his way.

He leaned back and framed her face with his hands, bending his knees to look her straight in the eye. "I have a feeling there's something still wrong. What's worrying you?"

"Nothing time and loving won't fix," she remarked, wrapping her arms around him. When she kissed him, talk ceased.

Tuesday, Ashley kissed Ryan goodbye and they both headed to their offices before leaving town. Ryan wanted to have one of his pilots fly her to Houston, but she already had her tickets on a commercial airline, so she followed her regular plans.

The entire time they were gone, they talked on the phone whenever possible, but most of the evenings, she was busy with wedding plans until she fell exhausted into bed.

Saturday, when she left for the wedding, she had her bags packed and was ready to fly home shortly. She couldn't wait to see Ryan. It was a morning wedding, and in the middle of the afternoon, she caught her flight home.

She slept all the way there on the plane, and when she called Ryan upon landing, she didn't get an answer.

As she drove to the condo, her anticipation built. A red sports car was parked at the curb in front, and she wondered if he had company. Ashley struggled to bank her disappointment at not finding him home alone and waiting for her arrival.

Pulling into the wide garage, she was surprised that Ryan's car wasn't there. The red sports car must belong to someone at another condo in the area. She guessed Ryan would come soon, because he knew what time she planned to arrive.

When she stepped inside the back door, the alarm was already turned off. Surprised, since his car hadn't been in the garage, she remembered the sports car in front, realizing Ryan could have driven it, rented it or even bought it.

Her heart jumped with eagerness and she smiled.

"Ryan!" she called. "Ryan! I'm home."

As she rushed through the front room, she heard someone walking around. She stopped, frozen in shock to see Kayla emerge from the master bedroom.

Ten

Ashley couldn't move. Kayla stopped also and they stared at each other.

While she looked at the redhead, Ashley's head swam. Kayla held clothing in her hand and had a purse hung on her shoulder. She looked her usual beautiful self, with a skintight, deep purple blouse tucked into her short purple skirt. Her hair was swept up and pinned onto her head.

Kayla was the first to break the spell. "Ashley!" she gasped.

"What are you doing here?" Ashley asked stiffly, having trouble saying the words while the heat of anger flared.

Kayla didn't answer and they stared again at each other. Finally, Kayla shook her head and shrugged. "I've got to go. You're home early." She turned abruptly to head toward the front door.

Nausea threatened, and Ashley struggled against it.

"Why are you in our home?" she snapped, following Kayla who spun around.

"Why do you think?" she retorted. "I was with him here last night when you were gone," she said. "I left something behind, so I came to get it today. I expected to be in and out before either one of you returned home. He gave me a key long ago."

"Get out of our place," Ashley cried, hot with fury.

"I'm going," Kayla said, shrugging her shoulders. Her eyes narrowed. "You'll never hold him. Not even this early in your marriage. He won't settle with one woman, so you might as well adjust to it." She turned to rush to the front door, yank it open and slam it behind her.

Ashley's knees almost buckled and she clutched her stomach, fighting the threatening nausea.

Spots danced before her eyes, and she sat abruptly in the closest chair. She had no idea how long she stayed there, but then she moved woodenly, barely thinking, locking up and leaving.

All she could think to do was go somewhere quiet to reason this through, and try to cope with what had just happened, so she could decide on what she'd do next.

Her fingers shook when she unlocked her car and climbed inside, driving away swiftly, keeping watch for Ryan to appear. But she didn't see him, and soon she was on the highway, driving mindlessly away from their home, while she hurt all over.

Her marriage was as flimsy and unsubstantial as a house of cards.

Why had she trusted a charmer who had talked her into marriage? Her father had warned her. She had known she was going into something that had slim chances of succeeding. Ashley realized that Kayla had been telling the truth when she'd warned her before the wedding that Ryan would not be faithful.

He had switched on the charm and deceived her, and she had been as naive and gullible as a child.

Ashley hurt badly. She loved him. And now he would break her heart, because she wasn't going to live with a deceitful man who had blatantly lied to her and been unfaithful to her.

Anger numbed her pain, but the hurt went deep. She could never shut him out, because of the baby, so she'd have to plan how to handle the immediate future.

She swiped at her cheek, wiping away tears and trying to focus on her driving, not even knowing where she was or where she was going.

Realizing that she didn't know what part of Dallas she was in, she began paying attention to street signs, driving around until she found a major route and then getting to a highway to head toward Fort Worth. The first parking lot she saw, she pulled off and called Ryan on his cell phone.

The minute his deep voice answered, her hurt mushroomed, yet a tiny glimmer of hope still burned that Kayla hadn't told the truth.

"Ah, my day just improved a thousandfold," he said, sounding full of cheer. "Tell me you're back in Dallas."

"I am," she said.

"I don't hear much joy in your voice. Ashley, are you sick?"

"No, I'm not. Ryan, I have a question."

"Sure," he said, the pep leaving his voice as his tone became somber. "What's up?"

"I came home and Kayla was there," she said bluntly. "She said she has a key to your condo and she left some clothing behind. Was she at your condo with you last night, like she said?" Ashley held her breath, closing her eyes and wanting him to emphatically deny it.

"Listen, Ashley, you know—"

"Answer me. Was she there at the condo last night?" she said, disappointment crashing over her and hurt washing back stronger than ever.

"Yes, she was, but it meant nothing. This time you listen to me while I explain," he said.

"Don't bother. You've said enough. She was with you and that tells it all. I'll call you later. Until I do, you leave me alone." In spite of hearing his loud protests, Ashley ended the call.

She loved him, and her heart felt as if it were shattering into a million pieces. She didn't want to see Ryan or talk to him until she'd made some decisions about what she intended to do.

For tonight at least, she wanted to be where Ryan couldn't find her. As she started to drive out of the parking lot, her cell phone rang. When she saw it was Ryan, she ignored the call.

Continuing to disregard his persistent calls, she got back on the highway and drove aimlessly. Dazed, she again tried to pay attention to signs, but her concentration kept wandering. She drove through Fort Worth, heading west and finally seeing a decent motel, she pulled off the highway.

"How could you, Ryan?" she said aloud in the empty car. She was oblivious to the hot tears streaming down her cheeks. "How could you do that to us?" she repeated, reminding herself that he had never declared he was in love.

Kayla had been the one telling the truth all along. Ryan had said he could explain, but it was obvious he could spin lies that sounded plausible. Kayla had been there. She had a key, because she had lived there with him. The thought was odious, and Ashley wanted to move out as soon as possible.

She parked in front of the motel office and went inside to get a room.

As soon as she was alone, Ashley put her head in her hands and let her tears flow. She took a deep breath and tried to calm down. She also ignored the constant calls from Ryan.

"How could you?" she exclaimed aloud. "How could you do this? Damn you, Ryan Warner," she cried, and tears came again.

Ryan swore as he listened to the steady rings and knew Ashley didn't want to talk to him. He drove swiftly to the condo, disappointed when he didn't see her car. But he still went inside, going through all the empty rooms in search of her.

He continued calling her, to no avail. Frustrated, he stood thinking about where she could be. It was Saturday and her office would be empty. He phoned anyway, and not getting an answer, decided to see if she was there, locked up alone and disregarding his phone calls.

Before he could cross the room, the doorbell rang. Startled, he turned, and for an instant, hope flared that it was Ashley. But she wouldn't come home and ring the doorbell. He strode to the door, to throw it open and find Kayla there.

"What the hell are you doing here again?" he snapped. "You came by today and told Ashley you were here last night."

"Well, I was. And yes, I did admit as much, which was only the truth. You'll never be happy with her, Ryan. You'll—"

Fury shook him and he gritted his teeth. "Kayla, I told you last night and I'm telling you for the last time now, you stay out of my life completely. I regret I ever gave you a key. I'll have the locks changed so you can't ever interfere again, but we're through. I'm married and I love my wife."

Kayla laughed, while her eyes glittered. "I don't believe that for a second. You barely know her."

"I don't give a damn what you believe. Get out of my life and stop interfering. We're finished forever, and I wish to hell I'd never met you."

"That's harsh, Ryan."

"Damn straight it is, but I mean it. Now, stay away from me and my family." He stepped back and shut the door in her face, spinning on his heel to stride out the back to his car.

When he left the condo, Kayla and her car were gone, and he hoped it was the last he ever saw of her. He sped to Ashley's office. The entire complex was quiet, empty of people. Glancing at his watch, he saw that it was after six o'clock. Ryan knew from what Ashley had told him that all the offices and some of the shops in the complex were closed on Saturday, anyway. Those that didn't close shut down by five.

He circled the building to go to the back, disappointed when he didn't see her car. She'd given him a key, and he let himself in and switched off the alarm.

"Ashley," he called, while he stood in the darkened hallway and listened to the stillness. "Ashley!"

Silence enveloped him. He searched the deserted rooms and paused in her empty office while he stared into space. Where could she be and why wouldn't she at least talk to him?

He drove back to the condo, hoping she would cool down and come home. He'd had the cook set the table for a candlelight dinner tonight, and he tried to get things ready, hoping any second he would hear Ashley coming through the door, but there was nothing.

Frustration grew and he called a locksmith, making arrangements for new locks to be installed Monday, to keep Kayla out. Then he paced the kitchen and swore, calling Ashley again with still no answer.

Again he stared into space. He'd told Kayla that he loved his wife. But he'd never told Ashley any such thing. He hadn't stopped to think about it, but he'd known that he expected to fall in love with her. Yet he realized now that he already loved her with his whole heart.

Why hadn't he examined his own feelings? He should have told Ashley how much she meant to him, and that he loved her. He loved her, and he hurt and he wanted her home with him.

"I love you, darlin'," he declared to the empty room. "Come home and let me tell you." Why hadn't he acknowledged it? Ashley was incredibly important to him and his happiness. "Ashley, answer your phone," he whispered, calling her once again and listening to her recorded voice telling him to leave a message.

"Ashley, I want to talk to you. Darlin', call me," he said. "Ashley, I love you. You're the woman in my life." He clicked the phone off and swore, frustrated that he was talking into a machine. "At least listen to your messages, Ashley. Call me."

Ashley finally lay down and stared at the ceiling. Hurting over Ryan, she was numb, unable to think or plan. She didn't know when she fell asleep, but the next thing she knew the continual ringing of her cell phone woke her.

She picked it up, not caring, nor intending to answer, because she still wasn't ready to talk to Ryan. When she saw a familiar number, she realized it was either her dad or her grandmother. Glancing at the clock, she saw it was only half past five.

Even though her dad routinely was up by five, he didn't phone her at that hour. Worried why he might call at such an early time, she took the call.

"Ashley?" Ben said.

"Are you all right?" she asked.

"I'm okay, but I'm worried about you."

She let out a sigh of relief. "I'm fine. It's a lot earlier than you usually call, and when I saw it was you, it scared me."

"I didn't intend to frighten you. Honey, Ryan just left here."

"He's been there at our house?" she asked, astounded that he would drive to the farm.

"Yes. He said he was afraid that if he called, we'd tell him you weren't here, even if you actually were. He left about thirty minutes ago and didn't want me to wake you, but I told him that I would try to get in touch with you. I decided not to wait that long. Ashley, Ryan is terribly worried about you."

"I'm all right, and don't you and Grandma worry. Please don't."

"We won't, now that I've talked to you. Honey, Ryan spoke with me. He wants you to come home badly. You need to listen to his side of the story."

"I thought you warned me about trusting Ryan," she said, surprised at the change in her father toward Ryan.

"I did, but that was then. I had a long talk with him. He's worried sick about you and he needs to talk to you. He loves you very much. Go home and let him explain. Your grandmother and I are worried, too."

Certain her dad was wrong about Ryan's love, Ashley shook her head silently. "Please don't you and Grandma fret. I'm going home this morning and I'll call Ryan. You stop worrying."

"That's my girl. We'll stop stewing if you call him and go home."

"I will," she promised, amazed by her father's complete

turnaround. But then she realized Ryan had been with her father, and he could charm most anyone he wanted to. "Stop worrying. I'll talk to you later."

"Take care of yourself. I love you," Ben said, then ended the call.

She stared at the phone and, with a sigh, dialed Ryan.

"Ashley! Thank God you called me!" he exclaimed, his voice clear and strong and making her hurt more than ever.

"I just talked to Dad," she said stiffly.

"Where are you? I have to talk to you."

"I spent the night in a motel. I'm about to drive to your condo. In about an hour I should be there, and then we can talk," she said, feeling as if her heart was breaking and again unable to keep back tears.

"I'm on my way home from your farm. I'll try to get there as soon as you do."

"There's no rush, Ryan," she said, knowing he would speed back. "Goodbye," she said firmly.

Moving around listlessly, and exhausted from lack of sleep, she dreaded talking to Ryan face-to-face. She was still astonished by her father's reversal, puzzling over it, wondering if she should have waited to hear Ryan's explanation before she left. She'd believed and trusted him once. Twice was too big a stretch.

When she arrived at the condo, Ryan's car wasn't there. She entered the empty space and was assailed by memories of facing Kayla.

Ashley dismissed those thoughts, going to freshen up, showering and changing to a pale blue silk blouse and matching slacks. She brushed her hair and then heard a car.

She walked through the house and was at the kitchen door when Ryan charged in. "Ashley!" he called. "Ashley!"

She hurried forward as he came charging through the door. "Thank God you're here!"

Shocked, she stared at him as he crossed the room in long strides.

Eleven

Ryan had a day's growth of beard. His shirt was rumpled, barely tucked into his wrinkled trousers. He looked red-eyed, disheveled and distraught, something she thought would never happen, no matter what kind of crisis he had in his life.

He crossed the room to her, reaching for her, but she put her hand up to stop him. "Slow down, Ryan," she said stiffly.

He inhaled and then crossed the last few feet, wrapping her in his arms. He looked down at her.

"Ryan, let me go—"

"I don't ever want to let you go," he said gruffly. He framed her face with his hands and peered into her eyes. "I love you, Ashley."

Her heart pounded. She wanted to wrap her arms around him and believe him and kiss him, but she couldn't. "You were here with Kayla Friday night, just as she said you were."

"Will you just listen while I tell you why?"

"I don't think I'll care about the reason," she answered firmly.

"Yes, you will. She came by here. I didn't know she was coming," he declared, and his words were slow and precise, as if he wanted to make certain Ashley got every word he said. "I told her it was over forever between us, and to go. She left. That's the truth and that's all there was to it."

"Ryan, she had a key—"

"That's from a long time ago. She had a key to this condo at one time and I never got it back from her. Frankly, I'd forgotten all about it. I'll admit that I had a relationship at one time with her and still went out some with her, but once you were in my life, there's never been another woman. Not once. She's out of my life forever, and I kicked her out of here Friday night in about twenty minutes after she had arrived."

Hope flared that he told the truth. Ashley stared at him, knowing only time would tell. But she loved him, so she would accept what he said. He looked and sounded sincere. As she accepted his explanation, her heart pounded with relief. Joy ignited deep inside her, while her hurt melted away.

He placed his hands on either side of her face again. "Ashley, I love you, darlin'. I love you more than anything else, and I should have told you before now."

Surprised, she stared at him for about three heartbeats as his words poured over her. Then she threw her arms around his neck. His arms crushed her against him and he leaned down to kiss her, with so much passion she trembled.

He loved her! His declaration buzzed in her mind, while she kissed him as wildy as he kissed him.

Suddenly, she leaned away. "Ryan, I love you! I love you so much that I thought my heart would break."

"I haven't slept and I can't tell you how worried I've been. I didn't want to worry your dad and grandmother, but I was sure you'd probably gone home, when none of your friends here had heard from you."

"Oh, my! You called friends?"

"Matter of fact, yes. I'm sorry, but I was desperate to find you."

"I'll phone them, but later." She raked his hair from his forehead with her fingers. "Ryan, I love you with all my heart," she declared, pulling his head down again to kiss him, the rough stubble of his beard scratchy against her face. In minutes she raised her head. "I should've listened to you."

He picked her up while he kissed away conversation, and she wrapped her arms around his neck. In the bedroom, he paused. "I love you, Ashley. I should've told you sooner. I think I've loved you from the first, but I didn't realize it then. I know I've loved you since before the wedding, but I didn't stop to look at my own feelings. I should've let you know."

"You can make up for it now," she said, smiling at him.

"I love you, darlin'," he whispered. He set her on her feet in front of their king-size bed, and she was caught up in as much urgency as he.

They peeled away each other's clothing. Ryan held her away to look at her, taking in the sight of her, then pulled her to him once again.

Later, he placed her on the bed and he moved between her legs, taking her swiftly, frantically. They clung to each other and she squeezed her eyes closed.

"I love you, Ashley! Darlin', you're the only woman I've ever loved!" he exclaimed, groaning with his need, and then they both rocked together until release came.

Later, as they lay wrapped in each other's arms, he

turned on his side to look at her. "I love you. I can't ever say it to you enough."

Gazing into his green eyes, she warmed with joy. "I won't ever get tired of hearing you tell me. I've waited to hear you say it. I love you and I think I maybe have since a few days after we got back together at Jake and Emily's wedding."

"Then why the hell did you fight me so on marriage?"

"You didn't love me," she said, combing her fingers through his thick hair. "You'd take charge of my life, which you did. I'd lose my independence, remember? I think I've told you this before," she teased, drawing her finger along his rough jaw. "I didn't even want to acknowledge my feelings to myself."

"I just didn't stop to think how important you were becoming to me," he said. "I won't ever do that again. Hereafter, if I love someone—you, our baby, my family—I'll tell them."

"See that you do," she said, and they smiled at each other. "You look as if you had a sleepless night, but even so, you're still the most handsome man on the whole earth."

"Aah, I'm happy to hear that you think so. What's important is what you think." He gazed somberly at her. "Ashley, if Kayla ever tries anything else, ignore her. She's been out of my life since before I first met you. I'm sorry she was ever in it at all, but she's gone now, and soon I won't even remember her. I hope you don't, either."

"I'm glad, Ryan. I love you. I'm so glad you love me in return."

"We're starting out okay, darlin'. Last night was rocky, but that's over, and it's good between us. I love you, beautiful wife."

She thrilled to his words. "I'll never get tired of hearing you say it. And I'm going to tell you that continually."

He kissed her with joy and then lay back, pulling her close against him.

She began to draw circles on Ryan's belly and he turned his head to look at her. "Know what you're doing?"

"I think so. I'll see what happens," she teased, and he rolled over to straddled her and nuzzle her neck.

Epilogue

The hospital room held balloons and one large bouquet of white tulips and red roses. Ashley was propped on pillows and she held a baby tucked in the crook of her arm. "He's beautiful, Ryan."

"Baby boys aren't beautiful. He's a handsome little fellow. Benjamin Zachary Warner. I think it's a fine name. My dad was overjoyed and yours sounded the same way."

"He was." She watched as Ryan crossed the room and returned.

"This is for you, Ashley," he said, sitting beside her and holding out a package.

Surprised, she looked down at a gift wrapped in shiny red paper and tied with a large red-and-silver bow.

Curious, smiling at him, she unfastened the ribbon and pulled away the paper. She opened a box, to find another, and when she opened it, nestled on a bed of dark blue velvet was a gold bracelet with diamonds. She gasped at the sight of it, surprised he would give her such a gift.

"Ryan, it's gorgeous!"

"It's for you, my love," he said. "I love you, Ashley, and want to shower you with presents."

She placed her gift on the bed beside her and opened her free arm to him. Engulfed in joy, thankful their marriage hadn't crashed and burned, she held him tightly. "Ryan, this is good."

Before he could answer her, someone knocked on the door. She released Ryan, who smiled at her and then stood to cross the room. "Come in," he called.

The door opened slightly and her grandmother thrust her head inside. "Can we come in?"

"Join us and meet Benjamin Zachary Warner," Ryan announced.

Laura gave a cry of joy and rushed to Ashley. "How are you doing?" she asked after cooing over her new great-grandson.

"I'm fine," Ashley said, reaching out to hug her grandmother who leaned over and gave her a squeeze. When she straightened up, Ashley saw that her father had entered carrying a large bouquet.

"We brought you some flowers," he said, while Laura took them from him to set them on a table. He leaned down to give Ashley a warm hug and then straightened. "How's my girl?" he asked her, stroking his grandson's cheek.

"Doing just great," she declared.

"Here's your first grandson, sir," Ryan said, taking the baby from Ashley and handing him to her father.

With a broad smile Ben Smith took the sleeping baby from Ryan and held him. "Look at him. Isn't he a fine one!"

"I want to peep under his cap and see his hair," Laura said, pulling up the knit cap carefully to see thick, black locks. She laughed and looked at Ryan. "He has his daddy's hair." She bent over the baby again. "He's adorable!"

Ryan's dad and brothers came into the room. When they crossed the space to Ryan, Ben handed over his small namesake to Ryan's father, who took the baby carefully. "Here's Benjamin Zachary Warner. With both our names he has a lot to live up to," Zach joked.

Brett turned to Ryan. "Way to go! Good-looking boy!"

"Thank you."

"Congratulations, man," he said, clapping Ryan on the shoulder. "You're a dad! I can't believe it."

"You better get used to the idea."

Ashley settled back against a mound of pillows, enjoying watching the visitors, four tall, broad-shouldered males who, along with Ryan, were "oohing" and "aahing" over her new baby.

Her bed was littered with presents that Ryan's brother had set down, and she knew they would get back to the gifts soon.

Someone else knocked, and again Ryan headed toward the door. It was Jake and Emily Thorne and Nick Colton. Emily smiled and rushed over to the bed to greet Ashley, while Jake and Nick stopped to shake hands with all the men.

"Emily, this is my grandmother, Laura Smith. Grandma, meet Emily Thorne."

As soon as they'd greeted each other, Emily turned to Ashley again. "Congratulations," she said. "It's fantastic that your baby's here. I can't see him for all the men," she said, glancing around, "but I will in a few minutes, if I have to snatch him away from them."

Ashley smiled. "It won't come to that."

"Ashley!" Jake came striding across the room, greeting her and her grandmother warmly.

Minutes later, Laura waded into the middle of the men

to claim her grandson. She returned to join Emily, who was still talking to Ashley.

"Now we can look at our family's newest addition," she said with eagerness. "He's a peaceful little thing."

"So far," Ashley said, smiling at her son. Conversation swirled around her, while her grandmother held little Ben in her arms, talking to him. Emily leaned over him, and when a look of longing swept over her face, Ashley focused on her.

Ashley was startled to see that Emily didn't look as radiant as she had on her wedding day, yet that was to be expected when she settled into the routines of daily living. Ashley remembered Emily's confiding about the marriage of convenience, and wondered if the union was rocky.

She thought about her own marriage, and she glanced at Ryan, to find him looking at her. Her heart skipped beats, and she yearned to take their baby home to begin their new life together. Commencing today, Ryan, little Ben and she were a family. As she gazed into Ryan's green eyes, he smiled, and she felt a bond between them that grew stronger daily. She expected their marriage to last.

Nick was the first to leave, and when he turned away from telling her goodbye, he spoke to Ryan and Jake before going. She looked at the three men. They were all handsome, charming to be with and loyal to each other. She thought how they had helped each other achieve their millionaire status at such a young age.

The Thornes left as Jenna came, and then Carlotta dropped by and another friend of Ashley's. Some old family friends came, and then everyone was gone.

Ryan was staying in the room with her and helping with their son. She fed Ben and cuddled him and let Ryan have a turn with him. Finally the baby was settled in his bassinet, and Ryan pulled a chair close up beside the bed and took her hand as he sat down.

"I love you, Ashley. We have a fine, handsome son."

She raised Ryan's hand to her lips to brush kisses across his knuckles and think how fortunate she was. "He's a miracle, Ryan. And so are you," she added. His green eyes darkened while he took a deep breath, and his fingers tightened around hers.

"Ryan, come here," she said. "Just stretch out beside me and hold me."

"You won't have to ask me twice," he exclaimed. He lay beside her, taking her into his arms with care and gently brushing her hair away from her face as they gazed into each other's eyes.

"He's perfect, our little son, and I'm the luckiest woman on earth."

"And I'm the most fortunate man and daddy. I love you, Ashley," Ryan added solemnly.

"I love you, too," she declared, gazing into his eyes, which conveyed his joy. "Ryan, you were right. I'm better off married, and so is little Ben, with a mommy and daddy who love each other. You were right the whole time. You told me the day would come when I'd admit it. I didn't think it ever would, but it not only has, that day has arrived a lot sooner than even you expected, I imagine."

"You're sure?" he asked, searching her expression, curiosity in his voice.

"Absolutely," she answered.

"Ah, darlin', I can't tell you how happy that makes me," he said. "Ashley, I love you more than you'll ever know, but I'm going to spend my whole life trying to show you."

Gently, he pulled her closer, still holding her loosely so

he wouldn't hurt her or make her uncomfortable. He leaned closer to kiss her.

With her heart drumming, Ashley wrapped her arm around his neck and held him while she poured her love for him into her kiss, thankful she was married to him, knowing she loved him with all her heart.

"This is paradise, Ryan," she whispered, and then returned to kissing him, while her heart strummed with happiness.

* * * * *

Look for LAST WOLF WATCHING
by Rhyannon Byrd—the exciting conclusion in the
BLOODRUNNERS *miniseries*
from Silhouette Nocturne.

Follow Michaela and Brody on their fierce journey to
find the truth and face the demons from the past, as they
reach the heart of the battle between the
Runners and the rogues.

Here is a sneak preview of book three,
LAST WOLF WATCHING.

Michaela squinted, struggling to see through the impenetrable darkness. Everyone looked toward the Elders, but she knew Brody Carter still watched her. Michaela could feel the power of his gaze. Its heat. Its strength. And something that felt strangely like anger, though he had no reason to have any emotion toward her. Strangers from different worlds, brought together beneath the heavy silver moon on a night made for hell itself. That was their only connection.

The second she finished that thought, she knew it was a lie. But she couldn't deal with it now. Not tonight. Not when her whole world balanced on the edge of destruction.

Willing her backbone to keep her upright, Michaela Doucet focused on the towering blaze of a roaring bonfire that rose from the far side of the clearing, its orange flames burning with maniacal zeal against the inky black curtain of the night. Many of the Lycans had already shifted into their preternatural shapes, their fur-covered bodies stand-ing like monstrous shadows at the edges of the forest as they waited with restless expectancy for her brother.

Her nineteen-year-old brother, Max, had been attacked by a rogue werewolf—a Lycan who preyed upon humans for food. Max had been bitten in the attack, which meant he was no longer human, but a breed of creature that existed between the two worlds of man and beast, much like the Bloodrunners themselves.

The Elders parted, and two hulking shapes emerged from the trees. In their wolf forms, the Lycans stood over seven feet tall, their legs bent at an odd angle as they stalked for-ward. They each held a thick chain that had been wound around their inside wrists, the twin lengths leading back into the shadows. The Lycans had taken no more than a few steps when they jerked on the chains, and her brother appeared.

Bound like an animal.

Biting at her trembling lower lip, she glanced left, then right, surprised to see that others had joined her. Now the Bloodrunners and their family and friends stood as a united force against the Silvercrest pack, which had yet to accept the fact that something sinister was eating away at its foundation—something that would rip down the protective walls that separated their world from the humans'. It oc-curred to Michaela that loyalties were being announced tonight—a separation made between those who would stand with the Runners in their fight against the rogues and those who blindly supported the pack's refusal to face reality. But all she could focus on was her brother. Max looked so hurt…so terrified.

"Leave him alone," she screamed, her soft-soled, black satin slip-ons struggling for purchase in the damp earth as she rushed toward Max, only to find herself lifted off the ground when a hard, heavily muscled arm clamped around her waist from behind, pulling her clear off her feet. "Dammit, let me down!" she snarled, unable to take her eyes off her brother as the golden-eyed Lycan kicked him.

Mindless with heartache and rage, Michaela clawed at the arm holding her, kicking her heels against whatever part of her captor's legs she could reach. "Stop it," a deep, husky voice grunted in her ear. "You're not helping him by losing it. I give you my word he'll survive the ceremony, but you have to keep it together."

"Nooooo!" she screamed, too hysterical to listen to reason. "You're monsters! All of you! Look what you've done to him! How dare you! *How dare you!*"

The arm tightened with a powerful flex of muscle, cinching her waist. Her breath sucked in on a sharp, wailing gasp.

"Shut up before you get both yourself and your brother killed. I will *not* let that happen. Do you understand me?" her captor growled, shaking her so hard that her teeth clicked together. "Do you understand me, Doucet?"

"Dammit," she cried, stricken as she watched one of the guards grab Max by his hair. Around them Lycans huffed and growled as they watched the spectacle, while others outright howled for the show to begin.

"That's enough!" the voice seethed in her ear. "They'll tear you apart before you even reach him, and I'll be damned if I'm going to stand here and watch you die."

Suddenly, through the haze of fear and agony and outrage in her mind, she finally recognized who'd caught her. *Brody.*

He held her in his arms, her body locked against his powerful form, her back to the burning heat of his chest. A low, keening sound of anguish tore through her, and her head dropped forward as hoarse sobs of pain ripped from her throat. "Let me go. I have to help him. *Please*," she begged brokenly, knowing only that she needed to get to Max. "Let me go, Brody."

He muttered something against her hair, his breath warm against her scalp, and Michaela could have sworn it was a single word… But she must have heard wrong. She was too upset. Too furious. Too terrified. She must be out of her mind.

Because it sounded as if he'd quietly snarled the word *never*.

HARLEQUIN Romance

Western Weddings

Jason Welborn was convinced that his business
partner's daughter, Jenny, had come to claim her share
in the business. But Jenny seemed determined to win
him over, and the more he tried to push her away, the
more feisty Jenny's response. Slowly but surely she
was starting to get under Jason's skin....

Look for

Coming Home to the Cattleman

by

JUDY CHRISTENBERRY

Available May wherever you buy books.

HARLEQUIN
Live the emotion™

www.eHarlequin.com   HRI7511

nocturne™

THE FINAL INSTALLMENT OF
THE BLOODRUNNERS TRILOGY

Last Wolf Watching

Runner Brody Carter has found his match in
Michaela Doucet, a human with unusual psychic powers.
When Michaela's brother is threatened, Brody becomes
her protector, and suddenly not only has to protect her
from her enemies but also from himself....

LOOK FOR

LAST WOLF WATCHING
BY
RHYANNON
BYRD

Available May 2008 wherever you buy books.

Dramatic and Sensual Tales of Paranormal Romance

www.eHarlequin.com   SN61786

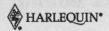
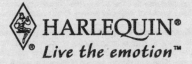

REQUEST YOUR FREE BOOKS!

2 FREE NOVELS PLUS 2 FREE GIFTS!

Passionate, Powerful, Provocative!

YES! Please send me 2 FREE Silhouette Desire® novels and my 2 FREE gifts (gifts are worth about $10). After receiving them, if I don't wish to receive any more books, I can return the shipping statement marked "cancel". If I don't cancel, I will receive 6 brand-new novels every month and be billed just $4.05 per book in the U.S. or $4.74 per book in Canada, plus 25¢ shipping and handling per book and applicable taxes, if any*. That's a savings of almost 15% off the cover price! I understand that accepting the 2 free books and gifts places me under no obligation to buy anything. I can always return a shipment and cancel at any time. Even if I never buy another book, the two free books and gifts are mine to keep forever.   225 SDN ERVX   326 SDN ERVM

Name _____ (PLEASE PRINT) _____

Address _____ Apt. # _____

City _____ State/Prov. _____ Zip/Postal Code _____

Signature (if under 18, a parent or guardian must sign) _____

Mail to the Silhouette Reader Service:
IN U.S.A.: P.O. Box 1867, Buffalo, NY 14240-1867
IN CANADA: P.O. Box 609, Fort Erie, Ontario L2A 5X3

Not valid to current subscribers of Silhouette Desire books.

Want to try two free books from another line?
Call 1-800-873-8635 or visit www.morefreebooks.com.

* Terms and prices subject to change without notice. N.Y. residents add applicable sales tax. Canadian residents will be charged applicable provincial taxes and GST. This offer is limited to one order per household. All orders subject to approval. Credit or debit balances in a customer's account(s) may be offset by any other outstanding balance owed by or to the customer. Please allow 4 to 6 weeks for delivery. Offer available while quantities last.

Your Privacy: Silhouette Books is committed to protecting your privacy. Our Privacy Policy is available online at www.eHarlequin.com or upon request from the Reader Service. From time to time we make our lists of customers available to reputable third parties who may have a product or service of interest to you. If you would prefer we not share your name and address, please check here. ☐

SDES08

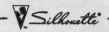

SPECIAL EDITION™

COMING NEXT MONTH

**#1867 BOARDROOMS & A BILLIONAIRE HEIR—
Paula Roe**
Diamonds Down Under
She'd been blackmailed into spying on Sydney's most infamous
corporate raider. Until he turned the tables and seduced her into a
marriage of convenience.

#1868 FALLING FOR KING'S FORTUNE—Maureen Child
Kings of California
This millionaire playboy was about to enter a loveless marriage
sure to make his wallet bigger...until a woman he'd never met
claimed to be the mother of his child.

#1869 MISTRESS FOR A MONTH—Ann Major
He will stop at nothing to get her inheritance. But her price is for
her to become his mistress...for a month.

#1870 DANTE'S STOLEN WIFE—Day Leclaire
The Dante Legacy
The curse of *The Inferno* left this billionaire determined to
make her his bride...and he doesn't care that she's his own twin
brother's fiancée.

#1871 SHATTERED BY THE CEO—Emilie Rose
The Payback Affairs
To fulfill the terms of his father's will, a business tycoon must
convince his former love to work for his company—and try to find
a way to stay out of her bed.

#1872 THE DESERT LORD'S BABY—Olivia Gates
Throne of Judar
He must marry and produce an heir if he is to become king.
But he doesn't know his ex-lover has already given birth to his
child....

SDCNM0408